MY GERMAN BROTHER

MY GERMAN BROTHER

||||||||||

Chico Buarque

TRANSLATED FROM THE PORTUGUESE
BY ALISON ENTREKIN

FARRAR, STRAUS AND GIROUX | NEW YORK

Farrar, Straus and Giroux
175 Varick Street, New York 10014

Copyright © 2014 by Chico Buarque
Translation copyright © 2018 by Alison Entrekin
All rights reserved
Printed in the United States of America
Originally published in Portuguese in 2014 by Companhia das
Letras, Brazil, as *O Irmão Alemão*
English translation originally published in 2018 by Picador,
an imprint of Pan Macmillan, Great Britain
English translation published in the United States
by Farrar, Straus and Giroux
First American edition, 2018

Owing to limitations of space, illustration credits
can be found on page 201.

Library of Congress Cataloging-in-Publication Data
Names: Buarque, Chico, 1944– author. | Entrekin, Alison, translator.
Title: My German brother / Chico Buarque ; translated from the
  Portuguese by Alison Entrekin.
Other titles: O irmão alemão. English
Description: First American edition. | New York : Farrar, Straus
  and Giroux, 2018. | "Originally published in Portuguese in 2014
  by Companhia das Letras, Brazil, as O Irmão Alemão. English
  translation originally published in 2018 by Picador, Great Britain."
Identifiers: LCCN 2017046938 | ISBN 9780374161200
  (hardcover)
Subjects: LCSH: Holanda, Sérgio Buarque de, 1902–1982—Fiction. |
  Fathers and sons—Fiction. | Illegitimate children—Fiction. | Berlin
  (Germany)—Fiction. | GSAFD: Biographical fiction.
Classification: LCC PQ9698.18.O35 I7613 2018 |
  DDC 869.3/42—dc23
LC record available at https://lccn.loc.gov/2017046938

Our books may be purchased in bulk for promotional, educational,
or business use. Please contact your local bookseller or the
Macmillan Corporate and Premium Sales Department at
1-800-221-7945, extension 5442, or by e-mail at
MacmillanSpecialMarkets@macmillan.com.

www.fsgbooks.com
www.twitter.com/fsgbooks • www.facebook.com/fsgbooks

1 3 5 7 9 10 8 6 4 2

MY GERMAN BROTHER

1

Insect wings, a ten *mil-réis* banknote, calling cards, newspaper clippings, scribbled-on scraps of paper, pharmacy receipts, patient instructions for sleeping pills, for sedatives, for painkillers, for flu tablets, for artichoke-leaf extract; pretty much everything is in there. And ashes; shaking one of my father's books is like blowing into an ashtray. This time I was reading a 1922 English edition of *The Golden Bough*, and when I turned page thirty-five I came across an envelope addressed to Sergio de Hollander, Rua Maria Angélica, 39, Rio de Janeiro, Südamerika. The sender was a certain Anne Ernst, Fasanenstrasse 22, Berlin. Inside the envelope, a letter typed on a tattered sheet of yellowing foolscap:

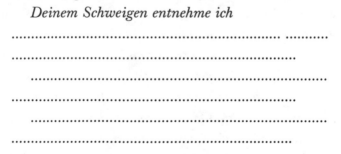

Berlin, den 21. Dezember 1931

Lieber Sergio
   Deinem Schweigen entnehme ich

Viele Grüße,
Anne

Written in German and teeming with capital letters, the only part I understand is the beginning and the name Anne in rightward-sloping handwriting. I know that as a single man my father lived in Berlin between 1929 and 1930, and it isn't hard to imagine him having an affair with a local Fräulein. In fact, I seem to remember talk of something more serious. I think a while back someone said something about a child he'd fathered in Germany. It wasn't an argument between parents, which a child never forgets; rather, it was like a whisper behind a wall, a quick exchange of words that by rights I couldn't have heard, or couldn't have heard right. And I forgot about it, as I shall forget about this letter in the book, which I need to put away in the back row of the double bookcase in the hallway. I need to put it in its exact place, as Father doesn't like me handling his books; much less this one. But I see Mother squatting at the foot of the bookcase, looking for a title Father has sent her to fetch. She won't take long, as it is she who organizes his library according to an indecipherable system, knowing full well that he'll be lost if she dies. And no sooner has she scurried to the study with her quick little footsteps, four thick volumes stacked under her chin, than I hurry over to put mine away. I know it was on that shelf above my line of sight, behind the Portuguese poets, a palm's width to the right of *La Comédie Humaine*, but it won't be easy to find its place again. By now the books have already spread out to press against one another at the back of the shelf; they seem to grow plump when confined. On tiptoes I push aside a Bocage in the front row, then grope the spines of the two Brits that were on either side of mine. There's something erotic about parting two tightly shelved books with my ring and index finger to force *The Golden Bough* into its rightful slot.

When I get to Thelonious's house he is waiting for me at the gate with a torch and a piece of wire bent at one end. We roam the tree-lined streets of the neighbourhood until nightfall, when we chance upon a Skoda conveniently parked on the corner of a poorly lit slope. I place my hands on the window like a pair of suction cups, forcing it down, and the glass gives about ten centimetres. Enough for Thelonious to stick the wire in, hook it around the lock and pull it up, which he's a pro at. I ask to drive, release the handbrake, let the Skoda roll down the hill and before I've even hit the kerb Thelonious is practically lying at my feet with the torch in his teeth and his head under the dashboard. He removes some parts that I can't see, connects some wires, and after a few pops and sparks the engine starts up. I accelerate, change gears, redline in second, make a tight curve, careen around the edge of the cemetery with squealing tyres, and as we head downhill towards the city centre Thelonious praises my manoeuvres with a grunt and a thumbs up, more concerned with rummaging through the glove box, the torch in his mouth. I think the best part of climbing into an unknown car, besides smelling its interior, familiarizing yourself with its quirks, sinking your backside into the seat, running your hands over the steering wheel and testing its responsiveness, is rooting through the glove box and finding, among other things, a document with the name, date of birth and photograph of the owner. I prefer it to be a man. I get more pleasure out of driving another man's car and I like to stare at the goofy faces they generally have on their documents. And I'd pay to see the expressions on their faces the moment they realize their car is missing, their mugs as they examine the mugs of thieves down at the police station. I feel a little sorry for the women, though, perhaps because I imagine them traipsing back and forth through the city unsure of where they left their cars, like frazzled mothers searching for sons who haven't come home. On Rua Aurora, Thelonious makes me pull over beside two old whores and asks if they'd like to get in, just to go for a spin in the car, no strings attached. He gives up on the working girls, jumps out, makes me scoot over and takes the wheel. He zigzags through cobbled streets to lose a police car that he swears he saw tailing us. But on an avenue in the East Zone that I've never seen before, he teaches me to listen to the car's engine, to feel its torque, to pinpoint the lapse during which it's possible to change gears without having to step on the clutch. It's a matter of downbeat and upbeat, he says, like jazz. He demonstrates the transition a few times, but what I hear is almost invariably the irritated squeal of metal on metal. We cross a railway line and, after a lurch, Thelonious discovers that the car is now forever stuck in third. He runs red lights, weaves around Sunday drivers, trying to maintain his speed until he is forced to brake behind a tram, which causes the engine to splutter and die. We abandon the Skoda right there on the tramline, which is no big deal as far as Thelonious is concerned, since it was already running on empty. We haven't any money for the fare and it takes us a good few hours to get back on foot because along the way there isn't a single decent car begging to be taken. We cross gloomy parts of town with factories, warehouses, tenements, closed garages and shops. We walk down crooked alleyways that lead us to a viaduct that ends in the centre of São Paulo, with its deserted streets, its skyscrapers in darkness. We then come to a traditional upper-class district, with English cars in the garages of houses that I've always thought too big for the land they sit on, which must seem even bigger on the inside than they do on the outside. And which, having such austere facades, must be fancier on the inside, more vibrant on the side where the people live. Climbing through the window of a house like that must be what it feels like for my father to open an old book for the first time.

It's after midnight when Thelonious and I part ways on the street corner between our houses, from where I can see the light on in Father's study. I climb the stairs holding my shoes so I won't have to give Mother any explanations, or wake her if she is asleep. In the hallway I catch a glimpse of the bookcase out of the corner of my eye and on the way to my room I pass the always-open door of the smoky study, where I think I see my brother and father sitting side by side. I get into bed fully dressed, then realize I've left the light on. But it's OK, I think, I can cover my face with the blanket, and underneath it's neither hot nor cold. It's a good place to think about my friendship with Thelonious, which reminds me of my father with my brother, who comes and goes from the study as he pleases but only reads comics, which reminds me that one day I might reveal to Father that I sort of managed to read half of *War and Peace* in French, and that now, with the help of an English dictionary, I was labouring through *The Golden Bough* before I came across the German letter, which, incidentally, reminds me that Thelonious, back when he was still called Montgomery, had another friend, Swiss or Austrian, whose parents sent him to boarding school, and without warning I am suddenly in an Oldsmobile with Thelonious, who is driving me to a boarding school called Instituto Benjamenta, where the Austrian or Swiss friend, a ginger-haired lad who has so many pimples his face is red and swollen, and this *Deutsche*-speaking friend reads the letter and laughs evilly with his monstrous mouth, with pimples invading his lips, with pimples on his tongue and gums even, and he really is an extremely sensitive, helpful young man, who translates Anne's letter for me very slowly, explaining the meaning of each word, its origin, its etymology, in a voice so soft I can't hear a thing, which sends me off to sleep.

2

I don't know what house it was, or if it was a hospital; all I remember is an unfathomable emptiness. And I see myself, still unsteady on my feet, frozen in the centre of a white-walled room. I had never seen anything like it and cried out when I saw my mother go over to the wall. I thought she was going to fall into an even emptier emptiness. I didn't see anything else after that. I buried my face in her bosom when she picked me up and didn't open my eyes again until we were home. Until then, for me, walls were made of books, without the support of which, houses like mine would collapse; even the bathroom and kitchen had floor-to-ceiling bookcases. And it was on books that I leaned, from the tenderest age, in moments of danger real or imagined, just as how today, in high places, I still press my back to the wall when my head begins to spin. And when no one was around, I'd spend hours sidling along the bookcases; my back brushing from book to book gave me a certain pleasure. I also liked rubbing my cheeks against the leather-bound spines of a collection that later, when they were at chest height, I identified as Padre António Vieira's *Sermons*. And, on a shelf above the *Sermons*, I read, at age four, my first word: GOGOL. I maintained this sensual relationship with books throughout my childhood, until the age of nine, ten, eleven, until the fourth or fifth shelf. I was even protective of my schoolbooks; it was a shame they came to me all grimy and doodled on by my brother. I'd head straight home from school with my manuals and compendiums, stopping only occasionally to visit Captain Marvel, who in addition to being my neighbour was also my best friend. I didn't feel as uneasy in his house as I did in others, with its walls covered in paintings and a veranda where we used to have the odd kick-about. But after a while I would grow anxious to see my library again; I even thought of the cockroaches with nostalgia. They'd appear from behind books, race across the spines from one end of the shelf to the other, and who knows if they felt on their bellies the same pleasure I felt on my back. I was always amazed to see the biggest cockroaches, hard-shelled and varnished, dart between two books where not even a fingernail would fit. Whenever I managed to catch one by the antenna, I'd go and show it to Mother, who would only tell me not to put the thing in my mouth. Mother was well acquainted with the cockroaches; when she married she knew full well what was in store for her. A less courageous woman would have done an about-turn the first time she set foot in Father's house. At that time, at the age of thirty-something, I estimate that Father had already amassed almost half of the books that he would acquire over the course of his lifetime. And prior to Mother, I imagine that this abundance of books, as well as piling up in the study, also cluttered up his future sons' vacant rooms like Aztec pyramids in ruins. Mother quickly had bookcases made to line the walls of the two-storey house, and when she fell pregnant she decorated the baby's room with books on linguistics and archaeology, in addition to the map collection, the Spaniards and the Chinese. For my room, two years later, she saved the Scandinavians, the Bible, the Torah, the Koran and metres and metres of dictionaries and encyclopaedias. When I was older, I saw the advent of three more double bookcases for miscellaneous or unclassifiable books, which Mother had installed in the garage since we never had a car, never any luxuries. Mother did the housework herself, and books were the sole indulgence that Father allowed himself. When he sold the printer's that my grandfather Arnau de Hollander had owned in Rio de Janeiro, he spent half his inheritance on rare books alone. The crown jewels of his library were eleven volumes ensconced in a niche in the sitting room, like an altar hollowed out of the middle of the bookcase, with a thick jacaranda frame segregating them from what one might call the plebeian titles. There used to be twelve of these rarities, but I managed to render worthless a sixteenth-century Hans Staden first edition. It was on the day my brother told me that when I was born Father had taken me for a mongoloid. I didn't even know what a mongoloid was; it was my brother's guffawing that got to me. I dragged over a chair, reached up to the niche and grabbed the book that looked the most sacred, because of the gold lettering on its hard cover. I tore it to shreds, page by page, and then peed on it. I was unable to tear the cover, and was about to set fire to it when Mother came and gave me a slap across the face, which didn't even hurt. But when Father came down the stairs holding a slipper, I shat my pants and pissed myself even though my bladder was now dry.

Just you wait, Ciccio, said Mother when, already grown, I asked why Father didn't write a book of his own, seeing as how he liked them so much. He's going to write the best book in *tutto il mondo*, she said opening her eyes wide, but first he has to read all the others. At the time, my father's collection consisted of about fifteen thousand books. In the end he had over twenty thousand. It was the largest private library in São Paulo after that of a rival bibliophile who, according to Father, hadn't read a third of what he owned. Supposing he'd been accumulating books since the age of eighteen, I estimate that my father read no less than one a day. And that's not taking into account the newspapers, magazines and his copious correspondence, including complimentary copies of the latest releases sent to him by publishing houses. Most of these he discarded after glancing at the cover or leafing through them quickly. He'd toss them onto the floor and Mother would gather them up every morning to put in the crate of church donations. And when something did take his fancy, he'd always come across some detail that would send himback to his earlier reading. Then he'd boom: Assunta! Assunta! and off my mother would go to fetch a Homer, a Virgil, a Dante, which she'd bring him, at speed, before he lost his train of thought. And the new book would be pushed aside while he reread the old one from cover to cover. It's no wonder my father so often fell asleep with a book open on his lap and a cigarette between his fingers right there on the lounge chair, where he'd dream of parchments, illuminated manuscripts, the

Library of Alexandria, and wake up distressed about all the books he'd never read because they'd been burned, or had gone missing, or were written in languages inaccessible to him. He had so much reading to catch up on that I thought it unlikely he'd ever get around to writing the best book in *tutto il mondo*. In any case, whenever I left my room and heard the clack-clack of the typewriter, I'd take off my shoes and hold my breath as I passed the study, giving it as wide a berth as possible. And I'd cringe if by some misfortune he happened to tear a page out at that very instant; I was sure that the rage with which he crumpled the paper, screwed it up in a ball and hurled it away was in part directed at me. On other occasions the typewriter would stop for Father to call for help: Assunta! Assunta! It would be some quote that he urgently needed to copy from a particular book. Thus it took him months to write, revise, cross out, hurl balls of paper, start over, correct, retype and, no doubt under duress, submit for publication what would be drafts of the bones of his magnum opus. These articles on aesthetics, literature, philosophy, or the history of civilization would occupy a newspaper column or a text box at the foot of a page. When Father died, we were approached by an editor who wanted to publish a collection of articles he had written over his lifetime. I was against it and went so far as to show Mother the profusion of illegible corrections and edits he had made to his texts or scribbled in the margins of clippings of his own articles. But Mother was convinced the book would be received with acclaim in academic circles, perhaps even published in Germany, thanks to the texts he had penned in that country in his youth. She even insinuated that I'd been trying to sabotage my father's work ever since I was a child, in view of one particular essay which would be missing from his complete works because of me. This was only half true, because it was my brother whom my father would occasionally entrust with an envelope to be delivered to the editor of *A Gazeta*, on the other side of town. For this, in addition to the tram fare, he would remunerate him with enough money for a week of milkshakes. But every now and then my brother would give me the tram fare and envelope, which I'd take to the newsroom on foot. I wasn't motivated by the money, which was barely enough for two sweets, but I was pleased by the responsibility of it all. The newspaper employees took a liking to me, and I didn't mind being mistaken for my father's sweaty courier, in whose hands they'd deposit a few more coins. But on one occasion, on my way to the newspaper, I stopped to play a bit of street football, which was common back then. Cars were few and far between, and when we saw them in the distance we'd shout: Here comes death! We'd scramble to fetch the lunchboxes, folders and jumpers that represented the goalposts and wait on the footpath for the car to pass before resuming our game. On this day it wasn't the traffic, but a sudden downpour that forced us to grab our things quickly and seek shelter under a shop awning. There was even hail, which we picked up, sucked on and hurled at one another; it was a riot. But suddenly I remembered Father's envelope, which I'd left under a jumper and which was now sitting there in the middle of all that water. I ran to save it and narrowly missed being run over, for that very second a

Chevrolet went past, snatching up the envelope with its tyre and only releasing it two blocks later. I went to retrieve the remains, but there was nothing to be done: Father's article was a strange grey mass, a wad of wet paper. Mortified, I lost all desire to go home. I whistled at Bill Haley's gate and he came out onto the veranda with a packet of his mother's menthol cigarettes. And for the first time he insisted on showing me the collection of ornaments he'd swiped from car bonnets, including a star from a Mercedes-Benz and a Jaguar's jaguar. It was cold on the veranda, my clothes were drenched, and I hoped he'd invite me in for a hot chocolate or something. I'd have stayed all night in that house full of paintings, but he wasn't too keen to let me in. I think he was ashamed of his mother, a painter and a divorcée who people thought was crazy. She sang arias at the top of her voice well into the night, and the neighbours said she painted in the nude.

3

In the early evening, Thelonious honks his horn down in the street aboard a brand-new Karmann Ghia, perfect but for a broken window on the right side. I'm forced to sit on one cheek, because on the passenger seat there's a constellation of splintered glass, along with a cobblestone, which I place on the floor. We're late to meet Udo, a friend of Thelonious's who is on holidays in the city after six months locked away in a Diocesan boarding school in the countryside. Thelonious has told me before about this German, the one whose parents caught him smoking marijuana, and who, to be precise, is from a country called Liechtenstein. He is waiting for us in a restaurant near the city centre, and Thelonious decides to leave the car in a quiet street nearby. He parks right in the middle of the street, which is a rather steep slope, and counts in English: One . . . two . . . one, two, three, four . . . We both jump out at the same time and he asks: Right or left? I bet left, wrongly, because it is to the right that the Karmann Ghia lurches, begins to roll and picks up speed, before slamming like a meteor into the boot of a parked taxi. On the next avenue over is the Zillertal, a large alehouse with a stage at the back where musicians and dancers are performing, the dancers in full skirts and the musicians in knee breeches with braces. Udo is at a table near the door and stands to greet us with a large mug of draught beer in hand. He hugs Thelonious, slopping froth about, offers me his left hand and says we've come at the right time, precisely as the band launches into the 'Liechtensteiner Polka'. He's about seventeen like us, but much taller, a really good-looking guy, very blond, who drags out his 'r's and at the end of each sentence puffs at the hair flopping onto his forehead. But no sooner are we seated than I feel like three's a crowd. I've ended up next to Udo, who addresses only Thelonious, seated in front of him, recounting some boarding-school antics that mean nothing to me. Now if Thelonious would only scoot half a metre to his right, we'd form a more impartial, equilateral triangle. But Thelonious, I don't know why he dragged me down here. He sits there quietly, nodding as his pal talks, chortling every time Udo stops to puff at his fringe. Thelonious of all people, who's always been the silent type, seems ready to laugh at anything today. He's amused by whatever old nonsense Udo comes out with: If there are no women, what can you do but have a priest. Facing an empty chair, all I can do is tap my feet in time to the music and observe the people around me: lots of fair hair and rosy cheeks, many undoubtedly of German origin. Which reminds me of the letter I happened across the other day, and without meaning to I begin to daydream about my father's secret romance in Berlin, already playing at searching the room for a German brother. He'd be a man of about thirty, most likely wearing glasses, with blond hair, a prominent chin, a long face, and a cone-shaped head. So far the only

15

person who partly fits the description is the trombonist, a fair-skinned redhead with full cheeks, as my father's would have been before he got old. But with the exception of the conductor, a dark chap with hairy legs, a bit grotesque in his knee breeches, the performers must all be second-generation, perhaps the grandchildren of Pomeranian immigrants who set up a colony in Espírito Santo, and I find it hard to believe that my brother has become a musician with a folk band in Brazil. I do think, however, that it would be perfectly natural for him, at some point in his life, to grow restless, question his mother about the origin of his name, insist on his right to know who his father is. And sooner or later, after saving a little, with or without her blessing, he would arrive in Rio de Janeiro with his father's home address in Jardim Botânico. It would not be hard for him to discover that Sergio de Hollander, having barely recovered from the losses, one after another, of Arnau de Hollander and Clementina Moreira de Hollander, had been hired as supervisor general of CAMBESP, the Administrative Council for Museums and Libraries of the state of São Paulo. In the white pages of the state capital he would find a Hollander Sergio de, but he would hesitate before dialling 518776, for the conversation was bound to be difficult. Our phone would eventually ring, and of that strange language Mother would only be able to make out the name repeated at the other end of the line: Sergio de Hollander! Sergio de Hollander! She would pass the handset to Father, who would lose his voice at first, then, his German rusty, would struggle for words, after which his eyes would grow moist, and in the meantime Mother would have understood everything and would weep along with him. And she would most certainly offer to have her stepson over for lasagne, receive him as her own son and, if necessary, put him up for a time in one of his half-brothers' rooms. For the young man's sake, Mother would even be willing to send to Berlin for Anne herself, who might have fallen on hard times in a country still affected by the war. And we would all live respectfully under the same roof, but an interval in the show and the audience's applause interrupt my flow of thought. I see that Thelonious and Udo have servings of sausage and potato salad before them, while I don't even have a knife and fork. At least the waiter doesn't stop bringing me new mugs of beer and topping up my glass of Steinhäger, which I use to toast my father, Anne, my half-brother, the cabarets of Berlin. Meanwhile, Udo continues to entertain Thelonious with his wisecracks: Got a skirt? Yep. Arsehole? Yep. It's all the same. Thelonious revels in it, he thumps the table, guffawing at the ceiling with his mouth full of food, and I'm embarrassed when an older woman at a nearby table looks at me with bulging blue eyes, obviously assuming I'm the crass one. She is accompanied by a bald gentleman, and together they make an elegant couple. She must have been a fine-looking woman in her youth, which takes me back to my father's girlfriend in Berlin. It's now clear to me that, after sending him letters and more letters, under the illusion that he would return to Europe, or at least give her and the child a home in Brazil, Anne would have felt abandoned. And when she discovered that Sergio had married someone else, an Italian at that, she'd have erased him from her life once and for all, torn up photographs and notes and under no circumstances would she have revealed his name to her son. But it is possible that, with conflicted feelings of pride and displeasure, she watched the boy grow up with an instinctive passion for books. He spent his days at the National Library, unaware that in its corridors he was imitating his father's strides. He avidly leafed through the same pages of poetry and prose that his father had never tired of leafing through. And when he arrived at contemporary literature, I want to believe that the young man, for no apparent reason, felt a certain unease. Unsure of his literary choices, he abandoned books without knowing why and, coincidentally or not, it was only then that his father's absence began to truly and deeply disturb him. No matter how he persisted with his reading, he felt fatherless in existentialism, among the New Novels, in nihilist poetry; he searched in vain for traces of him in books of more recent history. Only in dreams did he see his father, before the war, a faceless man among the pyre of books at the Staatsbibliothek, his hair in flames. In another dream he saw the same absent-minded man on the top floor of the library, reading *Faust* without eyes as the roof disintegrated over his head during the last bombardment. He never had been able to picture his father in military uniform, however, marching in the snow, rifle in hand, just as he also saw no reason for his mother to be ashamed of a husband killed on the battlefield. Then he swapped the library for synagogues, having gotten it into his head that he had Jewish blood. He rifled through every archive in his divided country, went by train to Warsaw, Budapest, Prague, returned home with G–d knows how many copies of files, thousands of names and even blurry photographs of Holocaust victims: Is it him? Is it him? Is it him? At which point Anne felt compelled to assure him: Your father set sail in 1930, safe and sound, for his native Südamerika. Then my brother hurried across town just days before they built the Wall and, on a scholarship from the Goethe Institute, flew to Buenos Aires, Montevideo, Porto Alegre, Rio de Janeiro, São Paulo, and he might even be sitting in the Zillertal right now, on the lookout for a Brazilian father who every now and then reminisces about his beloved over a beer in a German restaurant. Or else, finally resigned to the fact that his investigations have been a failure, my brother might now be piecing together material for an autobiographical novel in which he will invent a Brazilian father, not so different from his vision of the father he has never met. The fictional father will be a man of about sixty, probably short-sighted, his dark hair now greying, curly, as is common among Brazilians, but with a large head and cheeks, like himself. Perhaps he's even a mulatto, like the hairy-legged conductor with his arrogant jaw and cheeks that have sagged with age, exhausted from years and years of blowing into the trombone, the instrument inherited by his albino son, who, although he spits more than he plays, is the star of the band. Lost in such idle conjecture, I am surprised by Udo, whose face I have already forgotten. After I don't know how many beers and an entire bottle of Steinhäger, he finally deigns to speak to me: What about you, aren't you going to say anything? For lack of any other topic of conversation and inspired by my musings, I find myself saying that I have a German brother, that's right, a German brother. Udo is incredulous: Is this a joke? Now I have no choice but to elaborate: My German brother belonged to the Hitler Youth, he was taken prisoner at the end of the war at the age of fifteen or sixteen. And, what's more, I still have his mother's letters and a photograph of him performing the Nazi salute, with a swastika armband and everything. I don't know where I'm getting all this from; I think I'm mixing up details from several period novels I've been reading. But now Udo looks interested, he wants to know where my brother is now. In East Germany, I say, his mother's with the Stasi, the secret police. Envious of our common ground, Thelonious shakes his head: It's a lie, like hell he's got a German brother. I don't know what's with Thelonious; he and I have been best friends since we were children and now he's a stranger who only gives me sideways glances. A terrible silence falls over the table, until Udo leaps up, I believe with a urinary urgency, followed by Thelonious. Now that takes the cake, Thelonious keeping his towheaded friend company in the john. Minutes pass, I drum on the table and try puffing at my hair, which is stiff and doesn't move. Only then do I understand that neither of them has gone to the bathroom; the door on the right is the exit. The Zillertal gradually empties and the waiter prowls around my table, asks if I'd like the bill. After consulting the menu, I order a platter of *eisbein* with sauerkraut, another double draught and one more bottle of Steinhäger. As soon as he's turned his back, I too slip out to the right, passing a doorman in decorative dress, and race away. I sprint across the avenue and only stop to catch my breath on a parallel street, which as it happens is where we left our Karmann Ghia, which is now being towed away, boot-first, with the front all smashed in. I grab a taxi at the stand, and the Asian cabbie drives like a maniac. He weaves the wrong way up several one-way streets to the city centre, floors it to Rua da Consolação, zooms up the side of the cemetery honking wildly, and on the corner of Avenida Paulista, I ask him to wait a minute while I buy some cigarettes in the Riviera. I don't know how no one's realized yet that this bar has a back exit, which leads to a building raised on concrete pillars, where there is a nightclub called the Sans Souci. I've always wanted to see what the Sans Souci's like on the inside, have a few martinis, catch some jazz, but the bouncer asks for my ID. It's only a short walk home from here and I whistle the 'Liechtensteiner Polka' as I go, because it's hard to get annoying music out of your head.

Father's light is no longer on as I approach the house. I see two ghostly figures against the wall, Thelonious and Udo, who head for the gate and block my entry. We want to see the letters, says Udo. What letters? The letters from Germany. I push my way between the two, who can barely stand, but Udo immobilizes me with an armlock: Aren't you going to show us the letters? Thelonious says: I told you it was bullshit, German brother my arse. I try to worm my way out of it: The letters are very personal. I glimpse a set of brass knuckles in Udo's right hand, but it's only a silver keyring between his fingers. I put money on you, faggot, he says, and I'm not in the mood to lose a hundred smackers. I feel the ferocity of his words in his Steinhäger-and-potato breath. And I ask them to be quiet as we enter the house, because Father is given to bouts of insomnia, but Udo starts kicking chairs with his boots and Thelonious follows suit, imitating Udo's fake laughter. Then it's me who makes a racket in the hallway when I knock four Camões off the shelf. My fingers believe they've found the spine of *The Golden Bough*, but I can't seem to pull it out; it feels as though it's been nailed to the wall. When it finally does come, it brings two British anthropologists with it. I shake the book, a few ashes fall out; I don't think the letter is here any more, or maybe it never was, maybe it was a hallucination, but here it is, flattened between pages thirty-six and thirty-seven. I open the envelope and hand the letter to Udo, after locking the bedroom door behind us. Udo rocks back and forth like a clown-shaped punchbag, closes his left eye, his right eye, opens them both wide. He seems to struggle to understand what he's reading; as I suspected, he's probably forgotten all his German. He looks at the letter, looks at me, looks at the letter, looks at me somewhat aggressively, and now I wonder if I am the one who's been bluffing without realizing it. I understand that this Anne could be any German woman who knew Father vaguely, a librarian, a chatty neighbour; she could be, for example, his landlady in Berlin asking him to settle his rent in arrears. Udo plonks down on the edge of my bed, stares at the letter again, then sniggers. He asks for paper and a pencil, and says he's sorry he doesn't have a German dictionary so he can look up a few things. No problem, I say, right here on the bookcase in my room I have the *Duden* in twelve volumes. And, when all is said and done, considering his state of inebriation and his intellectual limits, Udo turns out a remarkably good translation:

Berlin, 21 December 1931

Dear Sergio

From your Silence I gather you are as always in your Books shipwrecked (immersed?). Desolate to steal from your Reading half a Minute, I write to inform you that our Son Sergio one Year of Age in excellent Health turns today. A Photograph I promise to send at the first Opportunity, and certain I am that yourself in the Boy's Mangokopf (mango head?) you will see.

If you don't mind, to the Subject of my last Letter as yet unanswered I return. Since that Day, Mr Heinz Borgart, the Pianist to whom I then referred, has demonstrated something more than Friendship towards me. For you until now I have waited, but you know that to give my Son a true Home I have always desired. Thus, if I do not receive a Reply from you within a reasonable Time, free I shall believe myself to consider the Hypothesis of tying myself to Heinz, who furthermore may even his Family Name give the Boy, who, in case you have forgotten, has on his Birth Certificate only his Mother's Name — Anne Ernst, it never hurts to remember.

Best wishes,
Anne

4

brothers-german: brothers who share the same
mother and father; full brothers

If my brother and I were to have a coin minted, showing
our heads on either side, and if we were to spin this coin
with a vigorous flick, we might glimpse Father's head
and Mother's head almost simultaneously. When the coin
came to a halt, however, we would once again be two
heads so unalike that no one would ever guess we were
brothers. Only frequent visitors to our home, or perhaps
someone studying one of the rare photographs that show
the whole family together, would see that we aren't
so much opposite as complementary. But Father's and
Mother's features were not distributed equitably between
us; my brother has a clear advantage. He has the facial
features of our father, who is far from handsome, but the
overall result is, mysteriously, a male version of our beautiful mother. The details I inherited from Mother are, on
the other hand, lacking in harmony; for example a pointy
nose without the high cheekbones to justify it, her full
lips that are unfitting on my small mouth. Her Italian
hair, which my brother now wears in long curls, is, on
my head, steel wool. And perhaps by some firstborn right

he got Mother's colouring, her green eyes and pink complexion, leaving me with Father's rough skin, underbite, grey eyes and glasses. To return to our point of departure: if the combination of my parents' faces was to be decided by rolling a die, we could have come into the world with myriad other faces, my brother and I, depending on the whim of the croupier, who, when it comes down to it, always decides in favour of my brother. Which is to say nothing of what was never up for grabs: his height of six feet, a good ten inches on me. However, with the toss of invisible dice, I think Chance compensated me with the gift of wit.

In the vicinity of an advertising school of dubious quality, in whose classrooms he was never seen, my brother earned a reputation as something of a pioneer. Countless female pupils went into his room as maidens, and left adjusting their underwear through their outerwear. I logged them all in a mental notebook, then, in the afternoons, I would track them down in the bars of Bela Vista, ask permission to sit at their table and introduce myself as my brother's brother. It was enough to make them put down their sandwiches or textbooks and give me their full attention, and over the course of our first conversation, I would gain their trust. I played the part of confidant and even stooped to pocketing love letters, which obviously never reached their destination. I also listened to their bitter complaints, because my brother was a prick who promised love and so on and so forth and then skipped out without a word. And I was amused to learn that few among them would have given him a second chance, had he sought them out, because he was too hasty, poorly disposed to foreplay, much less playing for extra time. As night fell we would exchange phone numbers, and, the next time we met, my brother would be of little consequence, because it was all Shakespearean sonnets from then on, and loftier. I know they listened to me, charmed less by the poetry than by the timbre of my voice, the one paternal characteristic in which my brother and I are twins. And it would be my trump card in the darkness of the cinema, where I had two hours to move, entertain and impress them with words my brother doesn't know, whether we were watching a *nouvelle vague* film or a romantic comedy produced by MGM. At the end of the show the lights would come up slowly and I hoped that, bit by bit, they would grow accustomed to my skin, my grimaces, that they would leave the cinema with my deep voice still in their ears and not be put off by my sweaty hand on theirs. It was from the Cine Majestic that I took home the first of my brother's exes, which gave me the satisfaction of cuckolding him, in a way. She was also the first woman in my bed, because until then I'd only done it in massage parlours. She was also the first woman I made come, come copiously, excessively, and scandalously, which made me suspect that she intended to reach my brother with her howls, wherever he was. When she left my room she dragged her feet in the hallway, glancing at the spines of books, contemplating my father in his study, and in the kitchen struck up an interminable conversation about cooking with my mother, who was making a strawberry pie. My mother was no fool, she knew very well what the *farfallina* was there for; there were always floozies hanging around, biding their time, hoping to bump into Mimmo. Wary of her husband's own youthful indiscretion, Mother would make the fig sign to ward off an untimely grandchild. But deep down she was proud of the revolving door in Mimmo's room. She resisted the urge to hang his bloodied sheets out on the clothesline, each time pretending to believe that the girls came to study the *Mappa Mundi* with Mimmo. Every now and then she'd complain about him locking the door, seeing as how she might need emergency access, should Father require a Cervantes, a Quevedo, a Calderón de la Barca. And because she was fair to her children, I believe she would, if she could, have divided Mimmo's women equally between him and his disadvantaged brother. As such, I don't know how she'd have felt if she'd known that my brother, having restricted himself to his own turf for a time, had been seen recently sniffing around Rua Maria Antônia, where I was taking a preparatory course for the Language and Literature entrance exam. It was fertile terrain for him, not because he was remotely attracted to Language or Literature, but because in this area of the humanities the female-to-male ratio was ten to one. I understood it the moment he set eyes on Maria Helena, and she struggled to believe me when I told her that that guy over there was my brother. And she couldn't understand why I refused to introduce them; she thought it absurd that two brothers weren't on speaking terms, she who, being an only child, had grown up resigned to talking to herself. But I never thought my brother would take a liking to her; in my class alone there were more than twenty supposed virgins, and virginity was a prerequisite he insisted on, quite the opposite

27

to me. I took it for granted that Maria Helena wasn't a virgin. I had yet to find out for myself, but she lived alone with her mother, didn't have a curfew, drank beer, and was tall and slender, with a tight arse, a certain *je ne sais quoi*, a free and easy way of walking, of speaking with open vowels, on top of which Maria Helena is from Rio and *cariocas* are notoriously more laid-back. She wasn't, therefore, my brother's type; her affinities lay with me. It was I who introduced her to Céline and Camus, and in exchange she lent me a Henry Miller full of smut. With her I could watch Godard, Antonioni and Bergman without having to explain the silences; I told her the story of my German brother, in confidence. I even invited her over to see Anne's letter, but she mistook it for a lame come-on and told me to take a hike. Maria Helena would get upset with me over nothing, the next minute she'd be planning marriage and children, then she'd go from peals of laughter to fits of rage; in other words, she was crazy enough to fall in love with me. Besides which, she was up for anything; she even went with me to Pacaembu Stadium to see Pelé play. And it was against the trees of Pacaembu that we would lean late at night for a little kissing with tongues, which was only possible if I balanced on their roots. I thought Maria Helena would give it up in no time, but it was a while before she even let me suck her breasts, and only through her bra, although she did once hold my dick through my trousers. This was around the time my brother started to haunt Rua Maria Antônia. Things were heating up between me and Maria Helena, and when I insisted she come upstairs with me, she agreed with the proviso that she might not

28

be ready to go all the way. Yes, she was a virgin, and the news came as a blow to me, while simultaneously reviving my worst fears, for my brother was still spending time lurking around the entrance to my school. He'd already laid five or six girls from my class, including the best pupil, who'd always struck me as very chaste. She was a fairly attractive country girl whom I'd started talking to, partly to annoy Maria Helena; I even invited her to the cinema once, right in front of Maria Helena. We went to see *The Exterminating Angel*, but she was too shy. She watched the film huddled in her seat and didn't find my observations funny. After I said goodbye to her outside the cinema, she followed me home without a word, head down, I'd almost say with her tail between her legs. I heard her sandals shuffling behind me on Rua Augusta, from Avenida Paulista to the slopes of Pacaembu, and from the front door to my bedroom, where she slowly undressed. In bed, however, of all my brother's former conquests, she proved the most insatiable. After that exhausting night she started dropping in unannounced, hunting me down in bars, and news of the affair ended up finding its way to Maria Helena's ears. But I didn't want to waste any more time with Maria Helena. I quickly hit on another classmate, then another, and another; if I could, I'd have drooled over every woman my brother had ever slept with. Until one weekend Maria Helena paid me a surprise visit in knee-high boots and a short skirt the likes of which I had only seen in French films. A shiver ran through me; for a second I thought she was dressed that way for my brother. But no, she made me stand on the first step, gave me a love

29

bite on the neck and told me how anxious she was to see my room. She even wanted to see the famous letter from my Mexican brother. In a husky voice she said she'd made up her mind now, she wanted me to be her first. She said other things along those lines, but right then all I could focus on was a collection of Italian plays on the bookcase at the foot of the stairs. It began to bother me, like a crooked painting, a provocative gap on the second-to-top shelf that was starting to get on my nerves. Look at that, I said to Maria Helena, who looked behind her and didn't see anything wrong. And ultimately it really wasn't anything serious, just one volume that had been recently removed from between two others, which were now touching at the top and not at the base, like two friends leaning in for a peck on the cheek without a hug. A fool might even have assumed the missing book was pointed, like a canine extracted from a crowded bite. As far as I could tell the absentee was a Pirandello, though only Mother could say for sure. I dragged Maria Helena into the kitchen to introduce her to Mother, who didn't take her hand because she was busy pressing a pastry crust into a baking tray. This time she was determined to get it right for her husband, who, although he appreciated her pies, never failed to remark, after *mangiar*ing them almost entirely, that they were a bit doughy. Mother was muttering this to herself, firstly because she too had been an only child, and secondly because she could see that Maria Helena wasn't paying any attention to her and had drifted off. That was when my brother barged into the kitchen. He stopped in front of Maria Helena and, with the tip of his finger, raised her chin towards him, as if he were an actor in a Western. Without taking his eyes off her, he grabbed a beer from the fridge, popped the cap off using the drawer handle, poured himself a glass and handed her another, his arm brushing my nose. I was pissed off and announced to anyone who would listen that I was going to buy cigarettes at the Riviera, where I drank three shots of cheap whisky without ice, smoked three cigarillos and vomited on the counter. I walked slowly down the hill, paced back up it, descended again and was startled by Maria Helena, who didn't quite collide with me as she was leaving the house. She was sobbing, and when she saw me she covered her face, slipped out of my arms and ran up the hill with her clothes all askew, the side zipper of her miniskirt in the middle of her backside. And, even all flustered as she was during that fleeting encounter, I desired her as never before, I pictured her as I showered, I couldn't sleep for thinking about her all night long. In the morning I picked a Flaubert to give to her as a present, not *Madame Bovary*, but *Sentimental Education*. As it happened, though, Maria Helena never came to class again, and only a long time later did I hear she'd been accepted into Architecture. I called her at home, but each time the maid would tell me that Dona Maria Helena was in the bathroom. Around the twentieth time, her mother picked up and insisted that I stop harassing the girl. And one day Maria Helena sent a chauffeur to drop off a number of French poets I'd swiped from Father's library to lend her, from Baudelaire to Francis Ponge. It was Mother who received them, put them back in order and made me swear to leave Father's books alone once and for all.

A Sergio de Hollander,
com a longa admiração
e a amizade
do
Guimarães Rosa
Rio, 11. VII. 56

GRANDE SERTÃO : VEREDAS

5

Brag, braggart, show-off; my classmates were unforgiving when I flaunted my father's autographed books around the halls of Language and Literature. And even though I knew it would annoy them even more, I couldn't help casually dropping into conversation the names of the writers who frequented our house: João, Jorge, Carlos, Manuel. Sartre? I crowed in a philosophy class. He made a point of dropping by our place with Simone, on his way through São Paulo. But above all my peers disapproved of my apparently blasé attitude in a time of great political upheaval. Still in my first year, in an effort to redeem myself, I started showing up at the student union whenever there was a meeting, whether it was to discuss university reform, demand toilet paper in the bathrooms or elect strike leaders. To ensure I didn't go unnoticed I usually took with me a volume of *Das Kapital* from home and, leaning against the wall, pretended to read Karl Marx in German while the student leaders tore strips off one another at the front of the room. And I must say, I have fond memories of that union of ours, where there were also art exhibitions, poetry recitals, singing, cachaça and companionable young ladies. Parties went on well into the night until the days prior to 31 March 1964, when the military seized power. But that hardly came as a surprise, even for someone like me who wasn't in the habit of reading the newspaper. Shortly before that date, on a street corner just a hundred metres from the university, I spotted groups walking down the hill from the elegant neighbourhoods towards the centre of town. I decided to accompany them to pass the time, since, after attending a talk at the union on the Cuba embargo, I'd sat through two hours of German and could skip French Lit as I was ahead in the subject. As we walked, I saw bigger and bigger groups streaming from other streets, I saw candle after candle flickering on sills, I saw the elderly waving to us from windows, and in Praça da República tiny pieces of paper rained down on the crowd from the buildings. Bells were pealing in Praça da Sé, women with veils over their heads were counting rosary beads, and I thought I'd best leave before anyone saw me there, captivated by the religious hymns, patriotic braying and apocalyptic speeches in front of the cathedral. I pushed my way back up Rua Direita against the current of people, who looked at me disapprovingly, as if I was trying to go against their procession of sorts. And at the Viaduto do Chá some kids with slicked-back hair started harassing me: Agitator! Scum! Communist! They blocked my way, cornered me against the railing of the viaduct, and it was only then that I remembered the book I was holding, the second volume of *Das Kapital*, which I immediately dropped and began to stomp on. At that moment I thought I heard a volley of gunshots, but it was fireworks going off over near the cathedral. The green and yellow lights in the black sky gave me goose pimples.

We didn't discuss politics at home much, though as far as I know, Father had socialist leanings. He hadn't expressed them in public lately presumably because, as supervisor general of CAMBESP, he reported to a governor who sympathized with the regime. But on the shelves of the master bedroom, then an almost foreign territory to me, alongside more conservative theoreticians and the already somewhat passé Marx, there were works by Engels, Trotsky, Gramsci, authors whose work I scanned so I could quote the odd passage here and there. When restrictions were placed on the student union, the Philosophy, Science and Language and Literature students started to meet in nearby bars, where word of mouth kept us up to date on the anti-dictatorship protests that were held around the city now and then, obviously without the publicity or impact of the previous Catholic marches. And I, who'd never been one to carry banners or chant, I, who'd never been the sort to hang out in groups, ended up acquiring a taste for such events. I mingled with university and high-school students, met activists from left-wing organizations, and went arm in arm with artists, journalists, informants, malingerers, oddballs and brash young women with bare legs who reminded me of Maria Helena. On this very day, as I leave the classroom, I'm excited to see Rua Maria Antônia closed to traffic. On the first cross street there's unrest in front of a retailers' association building, and I think they've gone a bit overboard by cordoning it off. But the arrival of a military police van with wailing sirens attracts new waves of young men and women, who occupy the entire city block in a matter of minutes. As a consequence, four trucks with police reinforcements roll up shortly afterwards, and before I know it I'm caught up in the middle of a big hoo-ha. People start pushing and shoving, and a guy in a red beret whom I've never seen before turns to me and says: What are you doing here? Without waiting for an answer the imbecile removes his beret, and as he leans back I hurry to save my glasses from a likely head butt. But before anyone can pull us away from each other, we all turn to look at some police escorts on motorcycles accompanying a black Cadillac. It's Kennedy! someone says, but it can't be because Kennedy is dead. It's him! It's the senator! others say, it's Robert Kennedy! and beside me a girl shouts long live the Vietcong, her eyes full of tears. Photographers' flashes pop when, to the sound of booing, the American climbs out of the car, and he strikes me as a little young to be a senator, too thin and white, with the face of a neglected son. I think his pallor might be fear, but he smiles faintly and waves at no one in particular. And that's when an egg hits the head of a large man behind the senator, a black bodyguard who remains impassive, yolk dripping from his Afro. The officers lunge, batons swinging, at some kids at the top of the street and drag one towards the van, hunched over, arms over his head. In the meantime the American has gone into the building and the students have closed in on the van: Let 'im go! Let 'im go! Let 'im go! The driver starts the engine and some bolder youths start rocking the vehicle, undaunted by the blows to their backs. The driver now tries to back up, but stops in time to avoid running over the girls beating on the back door. Let 'im go! Let 'im go! Let 'im go! we all shout, and some officers pull the girls away forcefully, and it looks like they're going to get a clobbering. But no, instead, the officers open the door and release the guy, who is all but carried away in triumph. The egg-sniper is none other than my friend Thelonious.

I haven't seen Thelonious in years, not since that drinking binge at the Zillertal when things got all weird between us because of my German brother. At the time I was pretty annoyed, but after a few days I had gone looking for him and whistled at his gate in vain a few times. His mother was the only one who would answer the phone, and I would hang up because she kind of scared me. But there were rumours in the neighbourhood that Thelonious was doing a stint in detention after being arrested in a judge's Studebaker with a tall, blond accomplice: Udo no doubt. I wished I'd been in Udo's place when he was caught red-handed, that's how tight we were back then. I wouldn't have minded getting the shit beaten out of me with Thelonious down at the police station, having my head shaved like his at the juvenile court. We'd been thick since kindergarten, where he'd lent me marbles, eaten the guava pudding from my lunchbox and had gone by the name Bugs Bunny. Much later, by which time he was known as Fangio, sitting in his back yard at night, with an eye on the light in the attic where his mother was listening to opera, we'd have wanking competitions to see who could shoot his load the farthest. He was the one who arranged my debut in a brothel and then consoled me, saying the whore was a heifer and that everyone has days when they can't get it up. On another occasion I showed him the pus on the end of my dick and he was categorical: gonorrhoea. He was already seeing a urologist in the red-light district and got me a consultation at a discount, then showed me how to unroll condoms on my stiff cock. In other words, there were no secrets between us. If I hadn't mentioned my German brother to him earlier, it was because for me it wasn't so much a secret as something that still belonged to the more tenuous realm of the imagination. But after that night, when Anne's letter confirmed Sergio Ernst's existence, my German brother would certainly have become the topic of our conversations; I could already see us planning a clandestine voyage to Germany aboard a freighter. But, from what I heard, at the age of eighteen Thelonious went straight from the detention centre to live with his father out in the boondocks. Without a friend, I had no one to share the subject with. It elicited nothing but yawns from the girls of my fleeting acquaintance, and at university even the classmates I got along OK with turned their backs the minute I brought up my father's time in Berlin, thinking they were in for an earful of boasting. I could, for example, have told them in all honesty that in 1929 my father interviewed Thomas Mann in the sumptuous Hotel Adlon, on the boulevard Unter den Linden. But, not satisfied, it might have occurred to me to add that, in spite of his respect for Thomas, it was on that occasion that Father had stolen his girlfriend, with whom he came to have a son by the name of Sergio. And one night, in the middle of dinner, out of the blue, I blurted out: I wouldn't be ashamed to have a German son. Father sat there with his fork suspended in front of his open mouth, while my brother continued flicking through the issue of *Playboy* he had on the table, to the left of his plate. Only Mother, after a moment of surprise, spoke up: Ma Ciccio, who's ashamed of a Deutsche son? Dunno, I said, all I know is that Thomas Mann was ashamed of his Brazilian mother. It was a controversial statement, based on what I'd read, but I made it nonetheless in the hope that it might get a reaction from Father. He could respond that Mann himself recognized traces of his Latin ancestry in his style, or that his mother had inspired fine characters for his novels; in short, he could have said that I was talking nonsense. But *voilà*, a bridge would have been built between us, and perhaps from then on he'd listen to me from time to time, correct me, acknowledge me as his son in some way. Perhaps he'd even allow me in the sitting room like a visiting student on nights when his writer friends came over for an Old Parr and they'd stay up to all hours exchanging news, anecdotes, literary gossip. Mother would dotingly top up my whisky every twenty minutes, just like theirs, and late at night, when the guests had gone, Father might, in a gush of tipsy sentimentality, reminisce a little about Berlin. However, seeing as how he had gone back to eating his gnocchi as if I'd said nothing, I pressed further: It must have been because Dona Júlia da Silva Bruhns Mann, with her mixed indigenous and Portuguese blood, spoke loudly, laughed too much and flirted with all and sundry in the salons of Munich. At this point Father finally rested his fork on the plate and pushed his glasses up on his forehead, a gesture I imitated in the expectation that for the first time ever we would look each other in the eye. But no, it wasn't to me that he turned, but to my brother, who was showing him a *Playboy* photograph under the table: Look at that backside! Formidable, said my father, an extraordinary backside! And Mother plucked at bread-crumbs on the tablecloth, as she always did when she played dumb during meals. I never once caught Mother staring into space; I think she even slept with her eyes darting this way and that. And the way she kept tabs on the family's every move, I don't doubt that she knew more about my German brother than the child's own father did. But it was pointless trying to get her to open up to me, much as it had been pointless to try and force open the drawer of her nightstand, in which I assumed she kept painful relics. I believe that Mother, who'd insisted on a church wedding, would have backed out if she'd known that, in addition to being an atheist, he'd fathered a son in Germany. But once married, as soon as she began to put the house in order, she would have stumbled upon traces of Anne everywhere. Letters from Anne would have sprung from the pockets of an overcoat, she'd have found them lying about in the corners of the study, they'd have slipped out of the books she dusted. Letters in German that she would have sniffed from the first to the last line, some accompanied by photographs of a blonde woman holding a baby with a very large head. After cleaning up, Mother would have gathered together that woman's effects, planning to set fire to them, but not before waving the papers in Father's face. But she'd have realized just in time that in Sergio's hazy memory, the ashes of Anne's letters might come to acquire, little by little, poetic flourishes, while the cremated Anne of the photographs would become a sort of Marlene Dietrich. Instead, Mother preferred to organize a file of these mementos of the other woman and lock it in the drawer of her nightstand. If Father really wanted to look at something, he should not hesitate to ask her for the key.

I call Thelonious, wave my arms, whistle, then feel like an idiot trying to get a famous artist's attention. Stopped constantly for greetings and hugs, he looks anxious to get away from the tumult after his beating, understandably wary of the military police lurking nearby. But among the kids who have just taken a drubbing in his defence, I hear some already expressing a certain disillusionment at seeing him set free: So he threw an egg, big deal, it was the American who had them cut him loose, what a wanker, hitting the brother with an egg, I'd like to see him throw a Molotov cocktail into the army barracks. And the minute someone announces that Bob Kennedy is leaving, they all turn to the centre of the demonstration and Thelonious looks a little lost, glancing over his shoulder. I'm sure he sees me now, but still he ignores me and sets off at a brisk pace towards Rua da Consolação. When I catch up with him, he is aloof in the face of my effusiveness and he asks me to please stop with this business of Thelonious; he wants to be called Ariosto. At first it sounds weird, Ariosto, then I begin to vaguely recall his mother calling him that: Into the house, Ariosto! Bath time, Ariosto! But he's not in the mood for chit-chat today, and I practically have to drag it out of him that he's back in São Paulo for good after falling out with his father and dropping out of a rural university. In an attempt to pick up some thread of our past, I ask after his friend Udo and am left without an answer. His reserve appears to confirm the talk I've heard at bars, that Udo's father got him out of jail after an agreement with the chief of police, which caused some ill feeling among the rank-and-file officers. And that Thelonious, abandoned there among crooks and chicken thieves, paid for his crimes doubly: two sessions trussed up on the parrot's perch, waterboarding twice and I even heard that two prison wardens had had him up the arse, but that's just malicious gossip. I don't know if the barbarity of prison life messes with a person's head, or if it's just the fact that we've been out of touch for so long that makes me feel so strange now standing next to Thelonious, I mean, Ariosto. I still need to refamiliarize myself with his face, which in the darkness I can only see briefly lit by passing car headlights, or every twenty metres under lampposts, in that deathly yellow light typical of cemetery footpaths. And by the time we pass the first bars with their TVs on, as we pass a pizza parlour with a queue trailing out of the door, and finally the roar of Avenida Paulista, I am beginning to enjoy our silence. Beneath the neon sign of the Riviera Bar I propose a toast, but Ariosto replies: I would prefer not to. And as we walk the final downhill stretch home he tells me through clenched teeth about his recent re-encounter with his former friend, there at the Riviera. He says he was having a beer quietly at the counter when Udo came up behind him and started to taunt him: You back, Che Guevara? You pissed off with me, Che Guevara? After the fifth Che Guevara, Ariosto says he turned and said: Why don't you run off to Daddy the Nazi? To which Udo retorted: Better than your mother the whore, who my dad banged. He'd held it together up to that point. But then Udo puffed at his fringe, and that was when Ariosto snapped. He grabbed Udo by the hair, smashed his beer bottle on the edge of the counter and drew blood from that silken skin with a shard of glass, giving him a gash from his left eye down to his jaw.

A creaking floorboard catches Father's attention: Who's there? He must have thought it was my brother, because he falls silent as soon as I say my name. But when I pass his study door, he tells me to come in. I won't lie and say I've never set foot in here before; when he's not home I don't even think twice. It feels like breaking into a car, but this time it's like the owner is sitting in it, waiting for me. I tiptoe into the smoke and find Father in pyjamas, as he will remain in my memory, reclining on the lounge chair with his glasses pushed up on his forehead, a book in his hands and the butt of a Gauloises about to burn his fingers. Now he repositions his glasses in order to see me properly and coughs twice, always twice, then asks if I've been getting into his Kafkas. Never, I reply spontaneously, relieved because of this crime at least I am innocent. Then he wrong-foots me: So what are you waiting for? Me? I don't think I can read Kafka in the original yet. But even after three years of school you still haven't learned German? He pushes his glasses back up his forehead and goes back to reading a book called *Strahlungen*, which if I am not mistaken means emanations, luminosities or something of the like.

I go to bed still reeling from that short exchange, because as far as I knew Father wasn't even aware that I was at university. And with my thoughts elsewhere I forget to turn off the light, but it's nice here under the blanket, where I lie in the foetal position with my arms down between my bent legs, like a wake-up stretch in reverse. Then I stroke my face to see if sleep will come, and it's a relief to feel my skin free of pimples, which have left only small bumps and notches here and there. After so much grief, I think I'm actually becoming better-looking, as happens to those who are brought to trial without knowing why, according to Kafka, according to my German teacher. I also think I must have had a late growth spurt of a good few centimetres, which encourages me to go and look for Maria Helena, who it seems has gone to live with her father in Rio de Janeiro. It's the first time I've been in an aeroplane, which is actually a propeller plane that flies very low, chipping paint off the mausoleums in Cemitério da Consolação, which makes me complain about the pilot, who is Thelonious, rather, Ariosto, who loses his nerve and decides to crash-land his plane right on my street, in front of a bunker I've never seen before, in the basement of my garage, where he tips beer on the ground and teaches me how to make Molotov cocktails.

6

With the gate broken, our garage is like a public library whose doors are always open, a standing invitation to book thieves. But the individuals who seek shelter there from the rain or the scorching summer sun aren't literature buffs. These idlers kill time playing spoof, or reading the old newspapers piled up in a corner, sitting on the rungs of the stepladder that Mother uses to reach the highest shelves. But when they do me the favour of vacating the premises, I occasionally go in to browse the bookcases, where there's a little of everything, mostly gifts from foreign publishers who hold my father in high esteem. In a place of such an assortment of literature, as habitués of second-hand bookshops well know, the appeal is the possibility of happening upon a good book purely by chance. Or serendipity, like how, when hunting for treasure, one has the good fortune to stumble upon something even more precious. Today I see the usual suspects on the same shelves: a few dozen Turkish, or Bulgarian, or Hungarian, books which Father may want to decipher one day. Also still in evidence is a book by the Romanian poet Eminescu, which Father has at least tried to read, as can easily be discerned from the pages cut with a paperknife. There's an Arabic edition of *One Thousand*

and One Nights, which he hasn't read, but whose illustrations he has admired at length, as evidenced by the lines of ash between its colourful pages. I'm now able to tell how many times my father has read the same book, as well as calculate how many minutes he has spent on each page. I don't waste my time with books he hasn't even opened, including a select few that Mother has gone to the trouble of stacking at one end of a shelf, believing that they might yet redeem themselves. Many a time I have seen her at dawn taking pity on the books scattered across the floor of the study. She has a soft spot for ones with their authors' pictures on the front cover, which Father despises; he says they look like they're posing for cheesy album covers. This may be the case with the bespectacled writer I am holding in my hands without knowing why, an American by the name of Varian Fry. *Surrender on Demand* is the title of the book that Father rejected, despite the praise from New York newspapers on the back cover. The edition and the praise both date from 1945, and under them is an introduction to the work, whose author *risked his life to rescue some of the most prominent politicians, artists, writers, scientists and musicians from Nazi-occupied France.* Biographies and reportage aren't among Father's preferred literary genres; besides, he left Germany before the Nazis took over. But on closer examination I see that the cut of the book's pages is slightly less uniform than that of a virgin volume and realize that it has indeed been browsed, but quickly, as one flicks through a newspaper to find the horoscope or lottery results. More towards the end I make out a subtle fissure in the sheaf of pages, and it was here that

Father apparently found what he was looking for. Indeed, on page 236 I see that he has underlined in pencil a name at the beginning of the second paragraph: *Among the refugees to cross the Atlantic were the harpsichordist, Wanda Landowska, the psychiatrist, Bruno Strauss, the pianist, Heinz Borgart, the sculptor* . . . I don't immediately understand why one of so many refugees has been picked out, refugees who, in 1942, according to the author, set sail from Marseilles for the United States, Mexico, Cuba and Brazil. But then I dash up the ladder to double-check Anne's letter and verify that the pianist to whom I had paid no attention is none other than the prominent musician Heinz Borgart, mentioned in this book. Back in my bedroom, I run my eyes over the encyclopaedias occupying two shelves; scanning the spines of the German *Brockhaus*: *A–Arnheim, Arnika–Blavatnik, Blavatsky–Camelot*, I open the third volume with shaky hands: *Borgard, Albert, engineer with the Danish army; Borganzo, village in Italy; Borgarnes, town in Iceland*; and I can hardly believe it but here he is in a decent-sized entry: *Borgart, Heinz-Frederik* . . . With no patience for dictionaries just now, even if I don't know the occasional word, I can still get the gist: *Borgart, Heinz-Frederik (Berlin, 28 November 1902), pianist and composer [. . .] son of Dr Oscar Borgart and his wife Gertrude, maiden name Gorenstein [. . .] the father a well-known editor from a prosperous family [. . .] Jewish mother [. . .] Borgart showed a precocious talent at the [. . .] studying piano and composition under Professor Artur Schnabel and Professor Kurt Weill [. . .] won the admiration of a select [. . .] and a successful career in the*

47

1920s with [. . .] in 1929 he gave a series of recitals of Franz Schubert's complete works for the piano at Heidelberg University [. . .] in 1932 he taught at the prestigious Cologne conservatoire [. . .] the Nazis' rise to power was [. . .] he was fired from the conservatoire in 1933 [. . .] he managed, however, to move to Paris in 1934 [. . .] His mother and sister, who remained in Germany, perished at the Auschwitz concentration camp in 1943 [. . .] Heinz Borgart resumed his career in France, however [. . .] but meanwhile he applied for French citizenship [. . .] directed the La Sonata Music Society from 1935 to 1939 [. . .] in 1940 the fall of France brought great [. . .] again found his life at [. . .] in 1942 aboard a freighter in Marseilles [. . .] Casablanca [. . .] he disembarked in the port of Santos, Brazil, where [. . .] residence in the city of São Paulo. I hurry into the kitchen, where Mother is fixing a garlicky lunch, and in the pantry there is a shelf with recipe books, almanacs, guides to São Paulo and the phone book: *Borges, Borges, Borges, Borges,* directly above it is a *Borganti,* there is no Borgart, but farther along I find the address of the German consulate. Public enquiries take place in a smallish room at the consulate, where some twenty people are queuing in front of a blonde employee's desk. Most are German citizens who stoop to speak to her in low voices, and from what I gather they have problems with stolen, lost or expired passports. Walking up the side of the queue, I take advantage of a pause and ask after the consul in basic German, but the blonde replies in Portuguese that Dr Weis is on holiday in Bavaria. What about the vice consul? The cultural attaché? I insist that there must be someone there qualified to deal with exceptional matters, but she whispers that the consular secretary only sees people with appointments. She calls the next person in line and refuses to give me any further information, even when I tell her I am looking for Heinz Borgart. It isn't possible that she hasn't heard of Heinz Borgart; all Germans know Heinz Borgart; there must at least be an official register with his name and phone number. The employee dryly states that the consulate doesn't give out its citizens' personal details. A fellow at the back of the room, perhaps to support me, booms that his country's diplomatic services knowingly cover for war criminals all over South America. But another German who was already sighing loudly behind me snaps that Nazi-hunters should report to Interpol, instead of obstructing the queue at the consulate. An argument spreads through the room, and it's Nazi this, Zionist that, and the blonde tells me in a tearful voice that it's not her fault, her name is Lieselotte but she is Brazilian and from Santa Catarina. Feeling sorry for her, I offer her the apple that Mother gave me when I left the house, then I ask if she happens to have the yellow pages to hand: *piano*, *piano*, *piano*, I look for a teacher but all I see are piano shops, and all of a sudden I remember the music school near my university. By skipping lunch I can afford to take a taxi, but the music school isn't there any more, now it's a Chinese pastry shop, so I decide to trot down to the Municipal Theatre. There are no staff at the back door, where I can already hear the echoes of the orchestra, a frenetic symphony that suddenly stops. It starts again after a minute of silence, and from the wings I observe the empty seats in the penumbra and the intense light on the stage, at the opposite end of which the piano's open lid conceals the pianist's head. I steal softly onto the stage, sidle along the backdrop towards the right, and, as I'm passing through the kettledrum player's shadow, a mishap of some sort causes the conductor to bellow and throw his baton to the floor. I freeze, holding my breath, and for a while all that can be heard is the baton clattering at the violinists' feet. At least the conductor's fury isn't aimed at me; he's addressing the pianist, who fingers a few isolated notes, to which the conductor shakes his head, vehemently agitating his thick white hair. I think they are swear words in Russian that he bellows until a hunchbacked gentleman heeds his call, climbs onto the stage with a case and sticks his head into the piano's guts. The pianist starts hitting the same key over and over, and by now the conductor has left the stage, where a few musicians light cigarettes and others stand to stretch or head for the toilet. I take the opportunity to pick my way through brass, woodwind and strings to the piano, where I find a petite woman sitting on the stool. As soon as she stands to allow the tuner to sit, I ask if she is Maestro Heinz Borgart's disciple by any chance. Without even glancing at me, she heads for the wings and down a corridor where there are more doors than wall. Because she looks foreign, I repeat my question in French, in English, in Italian, as I follow her, and I am about to try my luck in German when she slams her dressing-room door. Back on the stage, I don't find any better reception among the musicians, who are blowing smoke, napping or making banal sounds on their instruments which drown out my words. They're probably ignoring me because I am only in shirtsleeves, although their ties are loose, their jackets grimy and their trousers as battered as my jeans. Only the last of the cellists is willing to help: ¿El pianista Enzo Borja? and he points with his bow at the piano tuner: *Habla con Lázar*, tuners all have big mouths. Indeed, over a coffee at a bar behind the theatre, Lázar reels off the pianos he has tuned, not only in São Paulo, but also in Minas Gerais and the South, even in the Municipal Theatre of Rio de Janeiro. From virtuosos to moneyed dilettantes, from spoiled young ladies to bohemians with cigarette burns on their keyboards, he gets called out to mansions, schools and honky-tonks, he fixes everything from Steinway grands to locally made uprights, he makes no distinction between classical and popular, he is chummy with jazz, bolero, tango, samba and bossa nova musicians; he reels off his clients' names one by one, but he has never heard of the German pianist Heinz Borgart. Jewish? You're out of luck, I know the whole community, I've been tuning the Hebraica's piano ever since the club was founded. Lázar moved to São Paulo in 1950 and can assure me that since at least then the pianist has not lived in the city. He doesn't believe that a famous European concert pianist could have adapted to a country with a tropical climate, where pianos need tuning every hour. Trust me, says Lázar, your guy got out of here as soon as he could; he's probably playing waltzes in a kibbutz. I thank him, pay for the coffees, and on the footpath outside Lázar insists on giving me his card in the improbable event that I do run into the pianist in question, seeing as how the market is full of untrustworthy Italian tuners.

But by now I have already persuaded myself that Heinz Borgart really did leave Brazil at the end of the war to remake his life in France, or to resume his successful career in Germany. Successful career? I wish the man luck, says Lázar, because most of us more or less lost our touch after the war. Or do you think I was a piano tuner with the Budapest Symphony Orchestra?

When I get home I check the date, 21 December 1931, when Anne wrote the letter to my father, unaware, it seems, of what was to come. In little over a year her husband-to-be would be out on the street, forbidden to give concerts or teach, and would seek asylum in France with nothing more than the shirt on his back. And at the age of three my brother would be bundled onto a night train, or a minibus, or the back of a truck bumping along tortuous highways, unable to comprehend why, precisely now that he was learning the declensions and word order of his demanding native language, he would have to go back to baby babble in somebody else's. But in no time he'd be singing 'Frère Jacques' without an accent, he'd be given a dog and a bicycle, he'd make friends, he'd be loved by some and cursed by others, who would call him thief, skinflint, heretic and stinky. Taunted for being stateless, he would love his city more than any Parisian; with the yellow star on his chest he would explore one by one its boulevards, avenues, streets, squares, bridges, passages, impasses, he would learn the name and the history behind the name of every public place on the map. And just when he was about to start investigating the metro lines, he would find himself in strife again, unable to understand what he had done wrong to deserve being shipped off on an overcrowded freighter to who knows what shithole of a country. And after arriving in São Paulo and finding the city small, rainy, ugly and lacking in history, after having his bike stolen and adopting a stray dog, after learning at high school how to say fuck off, after finding himself a goyishe girlfriend, playing street football, becoming a Corinthians fan and beating a *pandeiro* in a samba circle, he would have to pack his bags again, perhaps to go and serve in the army in Tel Aviv, or to tag along with his father on low-rent tours like a wandering Jew. Or not. Perhaps none of this happened, because it is possible that Heinz Borgart had to leave wife and child behind in his frantic escape. He would send for them, of course, just as soon as he got his life in order, but once in Paris, a young musician, you never know. Should this be the case, I prefer to believe that on the eve of their wedding Anne recognized the mistake she was about to make by marrying Heinz Borgart, especially the risk to which she would be exposing her son. And to safeguard Sergio Ernst's name, she'd have broken off the relationship without compunction, accusing him of failing to tell her that his mother was Jewish, of not making it clear that by becoming half Borgart, her son would, as a matter of course, become a quarter Gorenstein. She would never, however, let Father know about the break-up, so as not to spare him from the image of her, night after night, in the arms of a glorious artist. Yes, she would be hard up for money, but she wouldn't let Father find out, nor would she ever go begging for child support from a man who wasn't even there when his son was born. Sooner or later she would find a permanent partner, perhaps a modest man who loved her more than she loved him but who would give Sergio an unblemished surname. He would be, perhaps, a small business owner, an artisan, a clerk, an Aryan who, in good faith, sympathized with National Socialism, and who, together with Anne, would be proud of the boy standing in formation in the Berlin Olympic Stadium, singing 'Deutschland über Alles'. I no longer have any doubt that there really is a photograph of Sergio in knee breeches and a khaki jacket with a swastika on his armband, but this brother will be lost to me forever.

7

scontroso (It.): surly in nature, easily offended, petulant, truculent

Ever since his days as Captain Marvel, Mother has considered Ariosto surly, and she still refers to him as such: That *scontroso* friend of yours stopped by earlier but I didn't want to wake you. Where did he go, Mamma? How should I know, the *scontroso* got tired of waiting for you and went out with Mimmo. Mother must be mistaken, Ariosto has no reason to go out with my brother. My brother is the opposite of *scontroso*, although he's always complaining that life isn't easy for him these days. In the middle of a family dinner, he has the cheek to announce to Mother that there are no more chaste young ladies over the age of fifteen left in the city. And he has started hanging around outside high-school gates, where he always manages to sweet-talk some unsuspecting teenager with that voice of his, which is more irresistible than ever now that he's doing voice-overs for radio commercials. Even Mother has put a radio in the kitchen so as not to miss his advertisements for Palmolive Soap, Adams Chiclets: A dainty box of surprises, or Hercules Beer: A black hero at last. Ariosto must be tired of

55

hearing my brother's voice say: He who does not live to serve Brazil does not deserve to live in Brazil. And Mother is the only one who doesn't get that the *scontroso* will never see eye to eye with a radio announcer who records government propaganda. In any case I deliberately stayed in bed late, with my head under the blanket, sensing that my friend was waiting for me. He's sought me out with a certain regularity lately, but my post-grad studies consume me day and night. I am happy to say that I am well on my way to an academic career, although for now I limit myself to teaching Portuguese in the college prep course, which pays peanuts. Perhaps I'll even land a position on the university faculty earlier than anticipated, seeing as how some of the lecturers have been fired and others have quit in solidarity, not to mention those who have disappeared or fled the country. Many students have dropped out, too, and a climate of fear has hovered over university circles ever since the events of 1968, when the regime really cracked down. There are no more marches, red flags are punished with prison, and at the bars I visit from time to time politics is not discussed. On Sundays, for example, I have dinner at an Italian cantina on Rua Augusta where my brother ruled the roost for a while. There, one drinks more than one eats well into the night, and it isn't hard to find female company for the small hours. Such as, for example, a girl who is always playing a wooden recorder at a table at the back, and who years ago I spied climbing the stairs of our house. She's a bit of a bohemian, but what caught my eye at the time was the way her hips swayed, *à la* Maria Helena, hips which can no longer be seen under her Indian tunic as she leaves with her male or female lovers at three or four in the morning. And yesterday at around that time, when I saw her sitting at her table, unspoken for, I introduced myself as my brother's brother while she played 'Eleanor Rigby'. To try and get a smile out of her, I even recited my brother's commercial in my best radio voice: Rádio Difusora AM, São Paulo, nine hundred and sixty kilohertz. Her name was Caramel and she couldn't remember my brother for the life of her, proof that her sexual initiation hadn't been especially memorable. I proposed a Chilean wine, seeing as how there was only a glass of water on her table, but instead of the wine she said she'd accept a chocolate ice cream. She wasn't waiting for anyone, nor did she mind staying there alone with her recorder until six o'clock in the morning, when her boarding house opened its doors. But it was cool, she could come with me, as long as it was OK for her to have a joint at my place. I preferred not to smoke pot on a first date because I'm not really in the habit; marijuana doesn't always help me achieve nirvana. But no sooner had Caramel set foot in my room than she lifted up her garment, showing a fine pair of thighs, albeit skinny and a little hairy, and pulled an already charred joint out of her knickers. It would have been rude of me to refuse, after she'd taken the first drag and, still holding the smoke in, told me in a voice that came out in a squeak like an old lady choking: Go for it. Soon she started to laugh, pointing at the foot of the bookcase, where four cockroaches lay writhing, belly-up, a common sight since Mother had discovered fumigation. The roaches reminded me of things I'd read long ago, and I don't know why I had to go and tell her that in the Polish gas chambers people had died gasping just like her, in the hope of finding a little oxygen above the insecticide. Not content, after another drag I told her that in their desperation the stronger ones had trampled the elderly, women, children, and Caramel waved her hands at me: What a downer! What a bad trip! Snap out of it! You see, every now and then I had obsessive thoughts about my German brother stuck in horrifying situations, but I wasn't going to tell her that. I just pulled my tattered copy of Anne's letter out from under the mattress and asked her to pay attention: *Berlin, 21 December 1931* . . . Caramel saw fit to play 'Yellow Submarine' as she listened to me read the letter, her fits of laughter creating tremolos in the melody. She found everything in the letter hilarious: my father immersed in books, mango head, and when I got to Heinz Borgart she put the recorder down and laughed even harder; she thought the pianist's name was too funny, almost the same as her old piano teacher's name. What do you mean, almost the same? His first name was different, it was Henri. I was surprised, because Henri is French for Heinz, and with that Caramel puckered up to play 'Yesterday'. I insisted: Was it Borgart? Was it Borgart? She stopped playing and whined: I don't remember properly, jeez, it was kinda similar, but it was a long time ago. Now you're going to have to remember, I said, clasping her head in my hands and shaking it: Was he German? Hey, you're not right in the head, it's getting light out, fuck this, I'm outta here. I apologized, offered to take her home by taxi, but at the very least I needed to know if the teacher was German. I dunno, I think he was French, now leave me alone, was all she said as she left. It was a lovely, cool morning, and I ended up walking with Caramel, who played 'Michelle' to the door of her boarding house, which was almost directly in front of a Catholic school called Des Oiseaux, just a stone's throw from my university.

A Portuguese lesson for a bunch of potheads requires no more from me than three hours of sleep and a cold shower. But today, after my all-nighter, I stand empty-handed in front of the class, not knowing where to begin. All I can think of is things we have covered in past lessons, anacoluthia, metaphors; the night unslept is a blackboard I forgot to erase. Through blurry lenses, or thousands of sleepless nights, I even see something of myself in the kid with the patchy beard sitting at the same desk I occupied years ago. And the brunette beside him is a mini version of Maria Helena, among so many other girls who also vaguely remind me of classmates from that time, like halfwits who take the same classes year after year. The only way to be heard over the racket that fills the room is to put on a deep voice and do a roll call, but at the moment all that comes to mind is the name Henri Borgart, Bogart, Baugard, Breaugard. And the pupils turn around to chat among themselves, just as my class did to provoke our Portuguese teacher, who was a bit of a nancy and ended up killing himself with a bullet in the mouth. I'm sure they laugh at my shoes, my second-hand watch, my ratty jeans covered in chalk and other gunk, which I never take off, the pockets of which I now start to pat. I suddenly jam my hand into my left pocket all the way to the bottom, and the piece of card under the box of chewing gum can only be the piano tuner's business card. It is indeed, and although it is somewhat warped and faded, having survived the odd trip through the laundry, Lázar Rosenblum's contact information is still legible. I abandon the bedlam of the classroom and race to the phone in the front office, but Lázar's wife tells me he's gone out, he's going to spend the morning looking after the piano down at TV Record. A famous popular music festival is taking place there, and Dona Dalila tells me about her favourite singers; she has even started to croon a romantic ballad when I cut the call short. After a twenty-minute walk I reach the auditorium, where I find a queue at the box office and a small crowd at the side door. It's the artists' entrance, protected by security guards, to whom I present Lázar's business card, after forcing my way through fans and kiss-asses. The card is passed from hand to hand, and a sweaty employee comes to tell me I'm not allowed in, because there's already a tuner on the stage. Yes, he's the one who sent for me, I say, full of pomp, passing myself off as the great João Gilberto's pianist. But João Gilberto doesn't have a pianist nor is he participating in the festival, according to the snitch behind me, so I slip over to the bar next door and order a coffee, which I drink standing in the doorway, one foot on the pavement. Every time I blink it takes a great effort to hoist my eyelids back up, and I am on my fourth cup when Lázar comes out of the artists' door. He throws a tantrum when I haul him off by the jacket; he no longer has any idea who I am, and his cup is still rattling on the saucer when I ask him

about a certain Henri, a French pianist with the surname
Borgat, Beaugars, or similar. He chases down his coffee
with a cheap brandy, which he throws back in one go
after tipping some out for his saint, and, looking bored,
pulls out of his case a bulging appointment diary bound
in turtle leather. But before he even opens it he slaps his
hand to his forehead: Of course, Henri Beauregard, an
exceptional client, he has not one but two pianos, which
he has tuned every month without fail, an Érard baby
grand and a full-length Gaveau. Having said all this, he
still has the audacity to deny me the pianist's address and
goes to put away the diary, claiming his clients' details
are confidential. I twist the old boy's arm and his open
case spews a handful of tools and a tuning fork onto the
filthy floor. On the verge of tears and more hunchbacked
than ever, he begs me with clasped hands to be careful
with his diary, which is already falling apart, and sheds
its pages as I hastily leaf through it looking for the letter
H. But it is under B that I find Beauregard Henri, Rua
Henrique Schaumann, 449, tel. 807246. I use the tele-
phone right there on the counter, which is jammed with
people in competition for plates of steak and onion with
rice and beans, it being lunchtime. And, even in the
middle of all that din, there is no doubt in my mind as to
the owner of the woman's voice that answers:

'Alu?'

'Anne?'

'. . .'

'Madame Beauregard?'

'Oui?'

Anne is reticent, probably trying to place the voice

addressing her in such an informal manner, because a stranger wouldn't use her first name straight up like that. And I think she might have forgiven the familiarity, if from the timbre of my voice she identified the person on the other end as a son of Sergio de Hollander. Perhaps at first she even thought it was Sergio himself calling her, an illusion that is dashed when I correct myself and address her formally in good French diction. But if Madame Beauregard really knew who was speaking, I would also understand if she felt outraged by the harassment via phone in her own home; after all, after twenty-seven years in the country, she'd have contacted Father if she'd wanted to. And I shudder to think that I was about to call her Frau Borgart, in response to which she would have hung up on me, and understandably so. I imagine that the Beauregards, like so many Jewish families, have radically severed ties with their country of origin. And from the sombre piano in the background, I assume that in that household Anne's romantic history is a taboo as untouchable as the atrocities of the war.

'Alu?'

8

At the Beauregards' address I find a house with closed windows, no sign of life. It is a modest building, almost touching its two neighbours, in a row of double-storey triplets, distinguishable from one another only by their colourings. The Beauregards' is ochre with green wooden shutters; the second-storey window is in the middle and the bottom one is on the left, in symmetry with the door. A piano like the one at the Municipal Theatre, however easy to disassemble, could only be taken inside by hoisting it over the top of the house, provided they dismantled the roof too. In a second phase, it would be carried down the stairs in the arms of natives little accustomed to such work, who would be further confused by the gestures of the husband and wife in a panic, he about the piano and she about the walls. Even so, it's hard to imagine a room inside that is large enough for one grand piano, let alone two. If I were the intrepid boy that I once was, I'd have jumped the low wall in front of the house and forced open the window to see for myself, and it isn't hard to imagine myself between walls that appear swollen, an effect created by mirrors, clocks, engravings, lamp holders and other hanging decorations. And perhaps I would be surprised to find two pianos in the sitting room with ample space, as one is sometimes surprised to see the deceased fit in a coffin that is too small. The pianos would be arranged lengthways, and continuing on I would discover how long the house is, which is hard to judge from the street. But first I would climb the stairs two at a time, and the top floor would be like a dark, narrow train carriage, at the end of which I would come to my brother's bedroom. Or, along the passageway there would be a succession of cubicles, like train compartments, to house a whole series of siblings, because there is no reason to believe that the Beauregards didn't procreate during their time in Paris, or even in Brazil. I do not doubt that they have produced children enough to erase the existence of the German son, who, unlike his uterine siblings, wouldn't study at the French lycée, wouldn't be allowed near the pianos, would take his meals in the kitchen and perhaps didn't even live there any more. But today, knowing that any slip-up will be fatal, I don't even dare open a rickety, lockless gate to set foot on the cement patio between the wall and the house, much less trespass down the side of the building to the backyard, where the family would be revealed to me, inside and out, by the clothes spread out along the clothesline. I stand stock-still in front of the house, and only now do I notice a flowerbed at the foot of the wall, where Anne's geraniums thrive. I am staring in amusement at her zinc watering can lying on its side, when a white cat jumps out of nowhere onto the patio and goes to lie on the doormat. Then I turn and see a couple appear at the corner, she with a handkerchief over her head, he in a chequered jacket. A little closer and I notice that he is wearing grey kid-leather gloves, as only a foreigner would early in the afternoon in a modest neighbourhood of São Paulo. She has a bag over her shoulder and is carrying a straw basket overflowing with lettuce leaves which isn't unbecoming. He, too, looks the part, with a bottle of beer in each hand and a stick of bread under his left arm. I couldn't care less that he is bald, for I've never given his appearance any thought; there wasn't even a tiny photograph of him in the German encyclopaedia. What takes me aback is her hair, which I can already make out under the handkerchief, completely white. Anne, the Anne I was expecting, was no more than thirty just the other day, although she is at least the same age as my mother, who, in contrast, ages inconspicuously. And when her blue eyes pierce me, I am convinced I have seen the couple before, one night at the Zillertal, when her few grey hairs made her look like a faded blonde. Today I'll limit myself to saying *bonjour*; at the most I'll offer to carry their shopping. I'll hold out my hand in greeting, not to beg. Come to think of it, I'll pay for a few lessons in advance, if the teacher takes on beginners, but, scowling, he quickens his pace to walk half a step in front of his wife, shielding her from my gaze. Arriving at the gate, he ushers her inside and I get the impression he's muttering strict orders through clenched teeth. She quickly takes the house key out of her bag and opens the door for her husband, who still looks like he's whispering the most terrible threats, such as, for example, that she'll turn into a pillar of salt if she looks back. But before closing the door Anne lets the cat in and glances at me furtively once more.

I look for a more discreet position when I begin to

suspect that they're spying on me through the slats in their shutters, which they keep closed with a light on inside. And, now, sitting on the neighbour's wall, I rub my eyes when I see a man crossing the street with mismatched footsteps. A drunk, I think, a German steeped in Steinhäger, or maybe just a tramp kicking a rat, but up close it's a boy with a limp and one built-up shoe holding a slender folder; a set of scores is my guess. He rings the bell, then pushes open the gate after Anne greets him from the door with a good afternoon which sounds, from a distance, almost accentless. A piano piece begins shortly thereafter and from a distance it, too, sounds pretty good, until it gets stuck in a particular spot and is restarted *da capo* several times. Then, after a longer pause, the music is reborn, flowing more smoothly than ever before, doubtless the artistry of Henri Beauregard and his Gaveau grand. To my untrained ears it is almost music in a liquid state, unmarked by fingers. I think it is a *berceuse*, and lulled by an assortment of melodies I take light naps over the course of the afternoon. More than blundering novices, I am woken by silences, just as I become agitated when I hear distant footsteps on the pavement, almost always pupils who trade places on the hour. Night has fallen by the time the coming and going ceases, and the music that now emanates from the Beauregards' house seems to lull the street, the neighbourhood of Pinheiros, the whole city. I am the only one who remains alert, perched on the stool of the Érard piano in front of the Gaveau played by the teacher, who looks at me and raises his eyebrows. I understand that he is inviting me to accompany him in one of Schubert's waltzes for four hands, but when I run my eyes over the keyboard I don't even know where C is. Just as well that Anne wraps her arms around me from behind and, slipping her hands over mine like gloves, leads me in copying her husband's finger work. And like a mother teaching her child to swim, she lets go without warning, keeping her hands nearby just to give me confidence. And off I go, after a hesitant beginning, when I elicit two or three testy looks from the maestro for touching adjacent keys. But soon I am performing delicate counterpoints for Henri Beauregard and am astounded to see how my fingers skitter from one end of the piano to the other. I weave my hands around one another, throw my left into the air, sweep the keyboard with the back of my right; with the pedals I prolong and dull the sounds as I please, as if playing with the accelerator and brakes of a newly stolen car. I no longer need to look at the instrument, I only have eyes for Anne, who points at the music rack, where there is a book of scores with a picture of Schubert on the cover. Anne now wants to teach me to read what I already know how to play, which in theory might be useful, as it might be for a writer to learn to read his book as he writes it. Or she'll demand I follow the score to the letter, because by now I am improvising with abandon, creating new directions for the waltz which I believe would make Franz Schubert himself proud. Once open, however, the book of scores turns out to be a photo album, on the first page of which are sepia images of my father arm in arm with Anne, who grows more and more pregnant picture by picture in the streets of Berlin, against a backdrop of the National Library, the

Pergamon Museum, the Brandenburg Gate. The next page, however, shows current photographs in Kodacolor that only Mother could have taken, of my father in his study smiling at the camera beside my Brazilian brother. There is also a black-and-white picture that Anne may have inserted at the last moment to please me, in which I appear as a child squatting with a football, while my brother sprawls across the arm of the chair where Father is sitting. The evidence that Anne and my father have never stopped corresponding leaves me so perplexed that I almost lose my place in the waltz. And Anne holds nothing back; she confesses that in secret she pays Sergio after-hours visits at the Museu do Ipiranga, where he is the director and so has all the keys. I become alarmed because she blurts it all out in German and in a tone sharper than the highest sharp of the pianos, but her husband continues playing with his eyes closed, enraptured by his own music, or delighting in my flourishes as if they were his. And there follow pages and pages of the lovers posing in the auditorium of the museum, or holding hands in a Tilbury carriage, or embracing on a canopy bed. I think I might even have glimpsed Anne's whiter-than-white buttocks, during an unusual transition from E to D minor, when a rude voice interrupts my performance: What are you doing here? It's him, finally, my German brother, still young, very tall, very blond and charming with a vast scar on his left cheek brought to life by its keloid appearance, which looks like a crab in relief: What are you doing here? He shakes my shoulders with inordinate strength, which almost knocks me off the stool, which is actually the neighbour's wall, from which

I promptly get up. And the person harassing me is a swarthy man with a red tie and a set of brass knuckles: What are you doing here? I instinctively take off my glasses, sensing the imminent blow, but what jingles in his hands is actually a keyring, because he's the owner of the house on whose wall I have dared perch my arse. The only reason he doesn't hit me is because he is startled by a pedestrian who doesn't even look all that imposing, a man of my stature who's just walked by, whose neck is the only thing I can see when I put my glasses back on. I catch another glimpse of him in poorly lit profile when he opens the Beauregards' gate without ringing the bell. I think he has a big nose, a high forehead, glasses; he's carrying books, has the key to the house and it can only be him. It has to be my German brother.

Henri Beauregard ended his recital as soon as Sergio went inside, and now the two of them will be sharing a beer as they wait for the delicacies Anne is preparing. I imagine sliced potato, onions, I imagine roast lamb; I'm famished but I refuse to leave as long as there is still a chance that my brother might go out tonight. I see no harm in approaching him on one pretext or another: Excuse me, do you know where Rua Teodoro Sampaio is? Thanks, are you heading that way? Do you mind if I walk with you? This is a nice neighbourhood, have you always lived here? You don't say, German? I couldn't tell, your Portuguese is better than mine, but if you prefer we can speak in your language, *Wie geht es dir? Danke*, me? Never, but my father used to live in Berlin, his name's Sergio, you don't say, yours too? Sergio is such an uncommon name in Germany, are you going into the city centre? Then we can catch the same bus, I'm not bothering you, am I? On the way I'll tell you a family secret, can you keep a secret? Let me pay, one day I'll even show you the letter I have in my other pocket, promise not to tell anyone? Berlin, 21 December 1931 . . . A blue light flickers through the shutters now, and instead of Schubert I hear the sorrowful voice of a young man singing: *Olá, como vai? Eu vou indo, e você, tudo bem?* The Beauregards are no exception on that street, they too are watching the popular music festival on TV. But not for long, because soon the only light to be seen is the yellow light that filters through the shutters of the master bedroom on the second floor. In the bedroom at the back my brother might be getting ready for a party, although it is already past eleven. If he takes after our father, he won't be interested in flings any more now that he's nearing forty, but will be looking for a serious woman he can marry and start a family with. Father was around this age when he moved to São Paulo, about the same time that some relatives of Mother's arrived, fleeing Mussolini, with her in tow. It's curious that the war brought my father's two women to the same city from so far away, although with very different prospects. My mother's communist relatives had family ties to a certain Count Matarazzo, whose heirs wouldn't have denied them jobs in their factories. Even my mother would have had work, in a storeroom, let's say, where she would have demonstrated the same diligence with which she now arranges Father's books; Father, for whom she works overtime to bake pies and, for better or for worse, has borne two sons. But the Beauregards, in addition to the murky

70

future that lay before them, wouldn't have been so eager to bring more children into the world after all they'd seen and lived through. They'd have devoted their attention to Sergio exclusively, who with time may even have tired of being a beloved child without a rival, the favourite in a void, my brother without me. In this, in a way, he'd have been like Father, whose childhood was like a period of quarantine after his older brother died of yellow fever. But at least Father enjoyed a little independence in his late youth, and I doubt I'll ever know if it was homesickness for his country, for his language, his parents, his home, his books, or a strong premonition that brought himback from Germany sooner than planned. Or perhaps he received a telegram from his mother in more or less the following terms: SHOCKED TO HEAR AFFAIR GERMAN GOLD-DIGGER STOP RETURN IMMEDIATELY STOP MONTHLY DEPOSIT DEUTSCHE BANK ACCOUNT SUSPENDED STOP. Here's hoping the Beauregards have enjoyed good health and continue to do so, because in Father's case, nothing short of the death of both of my grandparents, from meningitis, in one fell swoop, would have led him to quit the family home for good. A lifelong hypochondriac, he moved from Rio that same week, landing himself a public-sector job in São Paulo through influential members of the literati who, under the illusion that they would be repaid with generous reviews, also put in a good word for him at the cultural supplement of *A Gazeta*. Or who's to say Father didn't come here unconsciously attracted by Mother's ample breasts, inherited from my maternal grandmother, the exuberant Donatella, who paid for her sins on the end of her Neapolitan husband's blade? This honour killing comes to mind the moment the light in the Beauregards' room goes off, and I am gripped by an absurd jealousy. I don't know why, but it torments me to imagine Heinz touching and playing with Anne under the sheets, after they have undressed in the dark. And straining my ears here beneath the window is pointless, if it is true that in bed the Germans are far more discreet than us Latinos. I wonder if in times gone by Anne discovered with a silent Heinz pleasures that Sergio had never given her with a commotion. And because jealousy is a tunnel that leads to a tunnel within a tunnel, I now ask myself if Anne didn't meet the pianist back in the days when she was going out with Father. And should my father have doubted Anne's fidelity, let alone the child's paternity, his abrupt departure from Berlin would be explained at last. When she gave birth, Anne would have at her bedsidea more complacent, or optimistic, Heinz Borgart, ready to adopt the child that he already considered his own. Ijust don't get why Heinz would allow a child of his tobe named Sergio, unless paying homage to the alleged father, following an examination of the baby's face and wiener, is an authentically German form of mockery. But on my way home on the bus, calmer now, I admit that it was excessive of me to suspect Anne of being so deceitful, Anne who in her letter to my father stresses how much the boy takes after him, and even promises to send a photograph soon. And now I am amused by my jealousy of Heinz, that is, Henri, who, pushing seventy like my weary old father, in bed with Anne, must kiss her on the forehead, if that.

9

'Alu?'

'Mrs Beauregard?'

'Yes?'

'Hi, this is Caramel's boyfriend.'

'Caramel? Who's Caramel?'

I'm not surprised Anne is prickly with strangers; looking after her husband's schedule must be a pain. Even if it isn't very busy, she has to give the impression that it is, claim that an opening this year is unlikely, demand payment in cash, ask how advanced the candidate is, and make it clear that Monsieur Beauregard does not waste his time teaching the basics. Nevertheless, I insist that he will remember his former pupil and, to soften Anne's heart, I explain that my girlfriend only quit her studies because of meningitis. Caramel is better now, thank God, and the doctors have recommended that she resume her normal life, her degree in philosophy, piano, swimming, as soon as possible. The most painful part of the illness is the stigma. You should see the way her less enlightened neighbours and even her classmates at university turn their backs when they see her. Until just the other day, at the Club Athletico Paulistano's swimming pool, members scattered the minute she appeared in a bathing suit. How horrible, says Anne, how horrible, and in the word horrible, perhaps because its roots run so deep, her foreign accent is strong. Now Anne says there's a chance of a slot next week, but the wait will be agonizing for me. I ask if there really isn't any way she could squeeze us in today, as I'd like to surprise my girlfriend on her birthday, but Anne is adamant, today is out of the question. I sigh and confess that I thought it unlikely, so unlikely that I have already arranged an interview for Caramel with a new teacher. Anne bristles; she wants to know who it is and runs off a list of seven or eight Brazilian pianists whom she names with contempt. Then it occurs to me to invent a musician who has just arrived from Leningrad, and out of nowhere the name Nastasya Filippovna comes to me. In the ensuing silence, I fear I may have overdone it, as Anne appears to be consulting her husband through the toilet door, given that immediately afterwards I hear a flush. But when she comes back she agrees to make room for Caramel later tonight, at eight o'clock. I have the cheek to ask if at that hour the old maestro won't be tired. I also explain that some patience will be required with Caramel, as the meningitis has left some after-effects.

Before she beat me with a clog, I could have sworn that Mother left her bag open with her wallet on display on purpose so that every now and then I could help myself to five or ten *cruzeiros*. I never bothered to hide the theft; if I felt any guilt I wouldn't have left her wallet lying there, half open, sometimes outside her bag. And at the same ice-cream parlour counter where my brother drank his milkshakes, I ploughed into sundaes and banana splits unafraid of being found out at home. I thought it natural that Mother should slip me under the table, as a form of compensation, the perks that Father openly gave his firstborn. So I felt betrayed when she told me off. A trap set by one's mother is a terrible thing. The bruises from the clog blows weren't too bad, but her words stung for some time: Thief! Rat! *Rattone!* I took a dislike to women's handbags, even more so after Maria Helena dumped hers on my lap and asked me for a mint, her eyes glued to the screen. But the film was dark, and groping around I found pens, keys, a pencil case, lipstick, sanitary pads: everything but the mint. I did find some wads of paper, however, and I remain convinced that Maria Helena wanted me to open them from the very start. When the screen brightened during a close-up of Monica Vitti, I finally read the collection of torpedoes on the backs of illegal betting slips: Lose that dipshit babe! I'm gonna fuck you your hot! Nice snatch! And as if his poor language skills weren't enough, the scrappy handwriting was unmistakably my brother's. Years have passed and I am finally over these traumas, but now a leather bag comes along to set me off. It belongs to a student of mine, a girl from the south, who after class disappears into the toilets with a friend. I make my phone call to Anne Beauregard from the front office, smoke half a cigarette, glance around and slip into the ladies' room. I find what I expected: whispers and snickering from the cubicles and the air thick with marijuana. My intentions were honest, I was going to open them and tell, I was willing to spend half my salary on the material. But my student's handbag, agape on the counter, has left on display a roll of newspaper the size of an orange, the contents of which are no mystery. Pot couldn't have offered itself to me more explicitly, for on the crumpled page of *A Gazeta*, I can see the title of a column, 'Good News from Macondo', and the name of its author, Sergio de Hollander. I am about to grab it when my attention is drawn to a wallet beside it, half open, just like Mother's. Except that instead of banknotes with their usual dull colours, I see a scintillating sheet of cardboard with a red, blue and yellow clown on it, which at first I mistake for a joker from a deck of children's playing cards. But on closer examination, the clown is a mosaic of stamps, tiny squares that I've only seen individually. Once again I have serendipitously stumbled upon a prize even greater than the one I was after, not to mention more portable. I count some twenty-four hits of acid before tucking the sheet inside my Fernando Pessoa anthology, which has never been as useful in the classroom. I leave the toilets just in time to avoid tripping over a cleaner coming in, wrap the book in my jumper to protect it from the rain and arrive out of breath at Caramel's boarding house. I ring the doorbell several times before a sister opens the door a crack and sternly blocks my entry, as the house is for respectable young ladies only. Sitting on the doorstep, under the doorway that barely protects me from the rain, which is growing heavier, I wait one, two, three hours; to be honest, I didn't think Caramel woke up before midday. She wouldn't be able to leave the house now at any rate, because the storm has flooded the street; it even hails later in the morning. The asphalt is still wet, but the sun is out by the time Caramel appears in a pair of jeans as old as mine, except loose and lifeless for want of her former curves. She passes without noticing me and pauses a moment on the pavement with her wooden recorder pointed at a rainbow. She decides to go right, always keeping her eyes on the sky, as if using the rainbow as her guide, and I stop her just a footstep away from the corner. The cross street is blocked by two police vans and a bunch of officers with heavy weapons who are questioning passers-by and forcing drivers to reverse up the street. I tug on her arm, but Caramel shrugs me off and insists on continuing down that exact street. She seems determined to be detained at the barrier, where a sergeant inspects her recorder, then pats her armpits, breasts and sides, leaving me breathless when he lingers around her private parts. When she is allowed to go, Caramel disappears beyond the police vans playing her recorder, and if I want to catch up with her I will have to go around the block with great haste, especially because the officers are coming up the street, where I am the last civilian in sight. I quicken my pace now on the equally deserted street of the boarding house and I have the feeling that the patrol is already turning the corner behind me, although I had no idea Fernando Pessoa was a dangerous author. But a new platoon is staked out on the next corner, and I wouldn't be surprised if state-of-the-art sniffer dogs, hooked on lysergic substances, were to appear. My best option is to seek asylum in the boarding house, but, unmoved by my prayers, not only does the sister deny me entry, but she also threatens to call the Department of Public Order. They let me be for now, huddled in the shade of the doorway like a beggar asleep on the doorstep, and after a while I come to the conclusion that they wouldn't mobilize the national guard to come after a piece of shit like me, with scraps of narcotics inside a book of poetry. But I stay put just in case, I won't be taking my chances any time soon on a street that is so silent, way too calm. I can even hear the little birds at the nearby school, when a police van suddenly rounds the corner with squealing tyres and brakes. And it tears off, leaving a man crouching in the middle of the street, a black-haired kid of about my age. With his body tense and two hands on the ground like a sprinter at the start line, the kid looks from side to side, and at the sky with no rainbow. And with the first gunshot he bolts back towards the street he came from, perhaps to return to his friend's place, his girlfriend's, his mother's. Before the corner he stops short, swivels around, races back, and this is when the gunfire intensifies. I don't want to see his face, and I don't, because it explodes, his head explodes before I can close my eyes. When I reopen them I see the kid, who is still fleeing, but without his head; his headless body runs some ten metres, blood spurting from the neck, stomach and arsehole, and falls a short distance from the boarding house. Along comes the second police van, which is merciful enough not to crush his body, at least, before collecting it through the back door and driving off. I pull on my jumper despite the heat, but my whole body shakes anyway as I stare at the bright-red blood, diluted only in the puddles of water. Sirens wail, church bells ring, and the street slowly comes back to life; cars, pedestrians with their shopping bags, nannies with prams, a boy wearing the Brazilian football team jersey with a ball under his arm. I'm the only one who can't move, although I still need to talk to Caramel, who is God knows where by now. I ask a woman with a parasol what the time is, because my watch stopped at half past noon, but she looks at me in disgust. Instinctively, I raise my hands to my head and don't find it, but it must be because my hands are numb. My bent legs on the ground look as though they have no bones, the book weighs no more than the flies on my chest and my whole body is numb from the neck down, as if I've been shot in the spine. But even if I am crippled for life, I consider myself fortunate to have eyes to see the blue sky, the shreds of cloud, the pleated skirts on the girls from Des Oiseaux swinging back and forth. Life renews itself in my ears with the rustling of skirts and the song of a kiskadee, which isn't a kiskadee but a recorder, a recorder playing 'Hello, Goodbye'. And I throw myself on Caramel as if I love her deeply, as I will never love another woman. I kiss her on a lip, on the recorder, on her teeth, on a cheek, on an ear, on her hair, I mutter a string of words that I don't even understand. It's better this way, because if I told her what was going through my mind, she'd say I was disturbed, that I was on a mega downer and fuck this, what a pain in the arse. Caramel would be right, and during our embrace I see how the bloodstains on the asphalt are being erased by the rubber of Volkswagen, Ford Galaxy and Simca Chambord tyres. And even when my euphoria begins to wane, Caramel remains hanging from my shoulders, her fingernails piercing the weave of my jumper, perhaps

79

because right now she loves me too, above all things. Or perhaps it's because she senses the gift I have for her.

At the dining table, I recite to Caramel: *I want the flower you are, not the one you give. / Why do you deny me what I do not ask? / How brief even the longest of lives, / And our youth in it!* Like it? I'm not sure I get it. Read it yourself, then. When she sees the sheet with the psychedelic clown at the foot of the poem, Caramel's eyes bulge and her pupils dilate in anticipation. Even Mother thinks the clown is cute, when she comes in with two plates of reheated cannelloni. But the sight of the tomato sauce makes me feel queasy, and I snatch the book from Caramel's hands as I get to my feet: Not now, later. I leave her with the cannelloni and go upstairs for a shower; I need to be presentable to visit the Beauregards. With my wet hair momentarily straight, I comb it into the shape of a turban. Then I take a nylon stocking cap from a shelf under the sink, behind the African novelists, and work it over my head in circular movements. Wrapped in a towel, with my jeans in one hand and Fernando Pessoa in the other, I arrive in my bedroom, where I find Caramel stark naked on my bed. She is lying on her side, with a somewhat affected sensuality that unravels as soon as I appear. She points at the stocking on my head and almost dies of laughter, a clear sign that a roach made it through the frisking earlier. I wouldn't mind if she laughed at me until nightfall, because I'm not really in the mood for sex. But I can't refuse her now that she's summoning me with puppy-dog eyes, and when I lie down I try to remember her climbing the stairs with my brother; I almost ask her to call me by his name.

Caramel writhes beneath me, and it is with her legs over my shoulders that she comes, and comes for real, comes crying, comes scratching at me and comes very quickly. I have no illusions as to my sexual prowess; it is the expectation of other, higher sensations that have made her all wound up like this. I'm still lying lifelessly on top of her when she asks me to read that clown poem again. Later, I repeat, and she begins to doubt that she'll see the colour of an acid stamp before submitting herself to all manner of wild sex. I'm going to give you the whole sheet, my love, but not now, later. I put on the dress shirt and brown suit that belonged to my brother, which Mother took up for my graduation. I take off the cap and shake out my now dry, straight hair, which makes me look a bit like Ringo Starr in glasses, don't you think? Caramel says yes, but she barely notices my do, she just asks, with each minute that passes, if it's later now. Later is only after your piano lesson, baby. Piano lesson? Today you have a lesson with Henri Beauregard. That old bore? That's the one, honey. I'm not going. Yes, you are.

10

Carmela, so it was you? Anne kisses Caramel, wishes her a happy birthday, and the courtesy she shows as she greets me suggests that I am unrecognizable in a suit, tie and fringe. From his stool, sandwiched between the piano and the window, Beauregard welcomes Caramel with a strong French accent, for it appears there are truly no traces of German left in this household. In good French he says to his wife: This guy here, isn't he the same one who was prowling around the house yesterday afternoon? To which she replies: Yes, Henri, but this young man, in my view, he is harmless. At first it isn't easy to understand the layout of the living room, completely dominated by the two pianos that follow the concavities and curves of the walls. You get the impression that Beauregard and his pianos were there before the walls, which were built with precision, not by an engineer, but a tailor. There is only a little space left at the foot of the stairs for a mini sitting room with a TV cabinet, four chairs around a tiny table and a two-seater sofa where Anne has me sit. Then she slips between the pianos and the wall, brushing against some pictures of pastoral landscapes, and exits through a door at the back of the room. Meanwhile Caramel, who was already in a bad mood, scratches her backside when Beauregard tells her off for not bringing her notebook. She rummages through a pile of scores on the floor, picks hers, and instead of taking the same route as Anne, passes under the pianos on all fours straight to her stool. She seems put off by the teacher, as it takes her a while to get into the piece, which she plays like a child: using only two fingers on each hand. And observing Henri Beauregard, I wonder what goes through the mind of a man who before the age of thirty played with Kurt Weill, taught at the Cologne conservatoire and gave recitals at Heidelberg University, only to end his career in São Paulo, enduring an ill-mannered girl who plays the piano with four fingers. He is understandably cranky, and at the very moment that Caramel is beginning to show a certain confidence, he reins her in, tapping on the piano to keep time: Slower, Carmen! Andante, Carmen! Stop, Carmen! Stop! When the teacher starts playing the same piece with his eyes closed, I stand and sidle around the pianos, brushing them as I go, and open Anne's door to ask for a glass of water. Her face drains of colour and she takes two steps back, holding a knife and an onion, and the cat sitting on a stool doubles in size, white fur bristling. In my best French, I tell Anne *merci* for considering me harmless, and she suddenly blushes bright red: Pardon me, Monsieur, we had no idea you spoke our language so well. Don't worry, Madame Beauregard, I was touched by your consideration for Caramel and the generosity of your husband, who, to top it off, is treating me to this waltz by Schubert. Anne reacts to this almost with indignation, because the piece in question isn't a waltz, nor is it Schubert; it is Debussy's 'Clair de Lune'. I beg your pardon, Madame, as you can see music isn't my forte, literature is. I show her my book from a safe distance, afraid she might want to browse through it, but she serves me a glass of water from the tap and doesn't appear to be interested in Fernando Pessoa. She slices the onion in rings with dull thuds, and I'm still reeling off the poet's heteronyms when she says that her son's a bookworm, too, although neither she nor Henri are avid readers. *C'est la vie*, she says, shaking her head, and dumps the onion in the frying pan as she politely dismisses me from the kitchen: It was a pleasure to meet you, Monsieur . . . Monsieur . . . I pause, waiting for her to look at me: Hollander, Monsieur Francisco de Hollander. Anne stares at me, open-mouthed, examines my grey eyes, my cone-shaped head, my father's arrogant jaw, then looks away, rinses some spinach, begins to chop it into tiny pieces and murmurs that many years ago she had a friend with the surname Hollander. Her revelation is interrupted by Caramel, who hammers the bass notes on the piano and slams the lid shut with a bang. Bloody old pain in the arse! she shouts as she marches into the kitchen. She is determined to take the book from me by force, but suspends the attack when she sees the cat: Piaf, my love, my favourite little friend! She squats so that she is eye to eye with Piaf, who lifts her tail and ears, while Beauregard provides an encore of the previous night's melody on the piano. But you said something about a friend by the name of Hollander, ma'am? Maybe I know him. I have relatives who lived in Berlin between the wars. Anne opens the oven, closes the oven, fans her face, sautés the spinach and tries to remedy her slip-up with a muddle of digressions. She claims she has never lived in Berlin nor is she terribly fond of Germans, not least because her mother's family is from Alsace, which was once annexed by Prussia, like Lorraine, which she got to know as a young woman when she studied at the Nancy theatre school, where she was a colleague of Hollander, Ismael Hollander, a promising young comedian who was later sent to a concentration camp. Now Anne almost burns her fingers as she repositions the tray of pork ribs in the oven, and she begs my pardon for all of tonight's faux pas, such as alluding to Auschwitz in my presence. I have great respect for the saga of your people, says Anne, whom I reassure once again because I am not Jewish. Oh, well, then I'm doubly sorry, but in Europe Hollander is considered a Jewish name. Well, I don't know, it's never come up at home, we Brazilians are a very mixed people. At any rate my father, Sergio de Hollander, witnessed the rise of Nazism in Germany and as far as I know was never given a hard time. He was even romantically involved with a young woman by the name of Anne Ernst, from an excellent German family. Although I can only see her from behind, I am sure that Anne smiles, flattered, and this is when the maestro wraps up his number as an obvious signal for his wife to hurry up: It's been lovely chatting, Monsieur, I'm only sorry I can't invite you both to stay for dinner. You're always welcome too, Carmela, even if only to continue your tête-à-tête with Piaf. I'll show you out, she says, washing her hands in the sink, and as she dries them on a tea towel she gives a little gasp and a youthful skip: *Une minute*, Monsieur Hollander. She takes an apple-scented pastry out of the fridge and puts a slice on a dessert plate: You said your father lived in Germany? She hands me the plate covered with paper: It's my Alsatian grandmother's recipe, he'll like it. I follow her, sliding along the living-room wall, while Caramel crawls under the piano with Piaf, and Henri Beauregard takes refuge in the toilet under the stairs. I want to pay for the lesson, but Anne refuses to charge for fifteen minutes. I insist, I am adamant, otherwise I won't have the courage to ask the maestro to give Caramel another chance. I go so far as to take the money out of my pocket, but Anne acts offended. I try to drag out the goodbyes, step back to straighten some pictures on the wall, stroke Beauregard's piano, and I am praising its art deco design when I hear the sound of a key in the door and see the handle turn by itself. Paralysed before the door through which my German brother is about to walk, in my mind I run through all the fantastical ways I have imagined him since I found out that he existed. I recall the many times I have dreamed about him, with a different face each time, faces that morph in the aquarium of dreams, figures that vanish with the morning light, throughout all the years I have longed for this encounter. And now I no longer want the door to open; as far as I'm concerned the handle can go on turning forever. I prefer to continue seeing my brother in my dreams, his face still unfinished. I think seeing him at point-blank, with excessive clarity, will be like seeing a character from a novel that I've been conjuring as I read, detail by detail, suddenly splashed across the big screen. It will be like a spotlight thrown onto a character from a novel that I've been reading by candlelight, because the more indistinct their features, the better. If I could, I'd ask my brother to wait for me outside, to be once again the silhouette that I glimpsed in passing at night. But the door creaks, the handle returns to its original position, and what I see before me can't be my German brother. It's a man of my age, with slightly flaky white skin, Henri's hook nose and creeping premature baldness. He is truly banal-looking, the sort of person one struggles to commit to memory, who doesn't frequent dreams. This is my son Christian, says Anne in French, and this gentleman here, he is Monsieur Hollander, our dear Carmela's beau. Christian greets us with a nod, being weighed down with books, and bolts up the stairs two by two. Anne opens the front door, Caramel tugs on my coat sleeve, and outside I ask on an impulse: What about the other one, Madame? The other one? Your other son, Madame. I hear the sound of a flush, and even lit from behind I notice that Anne colours before responding: We don't have another son, Monsieur Hollander. She closes the door, and I am at the gate when she opens it again: *Psst*. It is to call Piaf, who was following Caramel and now scampers back inside.

 Standing in a crowded bus, I clutch the plate tightly after watching Caramel disappear into the night with my Fernando Pessoa. But I have that old feeling of having forgotten something; my hands are missing something but I don't know what. Perhaps I should have insisted on shaking Christian's hand; after all we have, or had, a half-brother in common. Through him it wouldn't be difficult to find out what happened to Sergio, if he ran away from

87

home, if he changed his name, if he brought shame on the family, if he is doing time, or if, as I fear, he is no longer alive. In this extreme case, I can imagine Christian telling me about his older brother with his heart in his mouth, not so much out of brotherly love, but startled at having come so close to death; a bolt of lightning that struck beside him. But it may also be that he has never heard of Sergio, who might have died when he was still a child, leaving his parents with a hazy remorse of sorts. An inexpiable sense of guilt that led the Beauregards to cloak the boy in a silence as thick as the one back at home, that no one dares break. But I have other silences up my sleeve, silences to negotiate with Anne during my next visits. She clearly wants me to return, otherwise she'd have given me the dessert on a paper plate, not on Limoges porcelain. Now that she has met me, she will surely want to know what has become of my father, but I won't satisfy her curiosity so easily. I'll just mention *en passant* his world travels, his marriage in Tehran, his silk business, his purebred horses, his amputated leg. I'll describe my mother's shot-silk garments, her enigmatic smile and one or other racier episode that I'll have to interrupt when I remember I have to be somewhere. The next day Anne will be at the gate waiting for me, pretending to comb the cat, but by that time I'll have forgotten the subject of Mother's lovers and will spend hours in the kitchen talking about my brother the plumber, his dark complexion, his almond eyes, his Muslim temperament. Until late one afternoon, with her back to me, Anne will confide that she was in love with another man before Henri. Slicing onions, to the sound of a lugubrious piano, she will tell me about the best nights of her life in Berlin, in the company of a foreigner who took her to dance the Charleston, a scoundrel who left her with a child in her belly and a bad taste in her mouth when he returned to South America. My father, however, for all intents and purposes, will be no more than a stranger to whom she sends pudding, as naturally as she serves pork to her Jewish husband. There are apostate Jews like Heinz Borgart everywhere, and it's not hard to understand their reasons. During the Inquisition, it is well known that converted Jews went as far as to accuse legitimate Christian families of being Jewish in an attempt to deflect attention from their own origins. But if Anne maintains that the Hollanders are Jews, I won't play tit for tat, nor will I go chasing down my family tree to prove her wrong. Not least because she could claim to have seen proof, first-hand, when she was intimate with Father, and I for one am not going to go and check if the old man is circumcised. It could also be that Father confided the secret to her as justification, or subterfuge, for refusing the child his surname. And it isn't his fault if Anne was reckless and quickly replaced him with another Jew. Perhaps she even has a predilection for Semites, so long as they're unorthodox, like Henri, or disingenuous, like Father, who devours Calabrese sausages with polenta on Sunday afternoons. And if I'm late for dinner on spaghetti alla carbonara nights, like tonight, I find no more than a few strings of pasta asciutta soaked in egg in the bowl, because he has already polished off the bits of bacon. At least there's enough bread to wipe the bowl with. I have barely taken a seat and the glutton is already sniffing the plate that I was going to give him later, for dessert: So what's that there? I push the plate toward him carelessly, and when he removes the paper covering it, Father practically drools: Apfelstrudel! I ran into an old friend of yours, she sent it, I say, not noticing Mother coming in with a pineapple pie: *Che amica?* Who sent it? Father takes a forkful of the apfelstrudel, closes his eyes as he chews and begins to mutter something like a prayer, oblivious to Mother fussing around him: There's pineapple pie for dessert, Sergio. The pastry is really thin. Father's eyes well up, and it is in German that he now recites: *Dawning in the bookshelves / are volumes in gold and brown; / and you think of lands traversed, / of images, of the garments of / women lost again.* Speak Portuguese, Sergio, speak Portuguese! begs Mother. Looking at her as if she were a new maid, Father orders her to go to the fridge and fetch a bottle of Liebfraumilch, a wine from the Rhine that he likes only because of its name. And he drinks the whole bottle, and recites all of Rilke's sonnets, and sings the waltz from the film *The Blue Angel*, and late at night I can still hear his baritone in the bedroom, crooning that lullaby that goes *Guten Abend, gute Nacht*: Good evening, good night.

DEUTSCHE GESANDTSCHAFT
LEGAÇÃO DA ALLEMANHA
SECÇÃO CONSULAR.
===
Rio de Janeiro, den 21.September 1932.

J.Nr. 771 III/31.

Illmo. Senhor,

Accusando a recepção da sua carta de 31 de Agosto
dirigida ao Bezirksamt Tiergarten, que encaminhei ao re-
ferido Bezirksamt, agradeço-lhe sinceramente o seu empen-
ho em favor da creança.

Com os protestos da minha mui distincta consideração

Addido de Legação da Allemanha.

Illmo. Senhor

Sergio de Hollander,

Rua Maria Angelica 39,

Rio de Janeiro.
=====================

11

A tattered book entitled *Il Martirio di San Gennaro*, a photograph of a woman with voluptuous breasts in an old-fashioned bathing suit, a photograph of the same woman dressed as a flapper with my mother in a tiny sailor suit and, inside a brown envelope, a letter to Father from the German Legation, dated 21 September 1932; a receipt addressed to Father from the same legation for 150 *mil-réis*, dated 3 April 1933; and a carbon copy of a typed letter, unsigned, whose text I translate from German as follows:

Rio de Janeiro, 31.8.32

Tiergarten Town Hall
Secretariat for Childhood and Youth, Child Welfare
Berlin
c/o German Legation

Dear Sirs
   The German Legation in Rio brought to my attention your letter of 27.5.1932, which informs me that my son Sergio, child of Anne Ernst, born in Berlin on 21 December 1930, is being maintained at the expense of the State.
   To resolve this situation, for which I am deeply

sorry and wish to find a solution compatible with my means, please allow me to present, with the consent of the Legation, two proposals concerning my son's future.

The first – the best, in my opinion – would be to have the child come to Rio, where he would live with my family. In the event that Miss Ernst should accept this proposal, it would, obviously, be at my own expense.

In the event that it is deemed unacceptable and the child remains in Germany, I will send a monthly contribution of 150 mil-réis, which is all I can afford at present.

In the hope that you will consider my proposals with benevolence, respectfully yours.

Whether Anne wished to rid herself of a shameful burden, was going along with a husband's pettiness, or had prevented a one-and-a-half-year-old child from gaining a family in Brazil out of sheer spite, it all pales in comparison to the cheek of sending Father a pastry via me. It would be easier to forgive if, still bearing a grudge against her runaway lover, she had sent him a poisoned apfelstrudel as revenge served cold. But as I put the documents back in the brown envelope, I find at the bottom a photograph not much bigger than a playing card, with the names *Sergio and Anne Ernst* on the back in my mother's handwriting. I stare at length at little Sergio, five or six months old, an age at which only a mother can say for sure who the child resembles. To me he is a baby like any other, except for his startled eyes, looking upwards. But the Anne smiling at the baby, even accounting for the distance of forty years, isn't the Anne I know. With a square face, sharp nose and peasant-like demeanour, the woman in the photograph looks less like Madame Beauregard than she does my own mother, like a first draft of Mother that Father set aside. Speaking of Mother, I can hear her downstairs now, having just arrived home from Mass: Sergio, *ti preparo un caffè*. I busy myself putting the papers back into the order I found them in, more or less, so she won't feel obliged to give me a scolding. But I leave the drawer open an inch more than it was, so she'll have no doubt that I've been snooping, as I believe was her intention. And even if it wasn't, she can hardly demand that I return the photograph of Sergio and Anne Ernst that I take with me: Photograph of who? I am convinced that during her sleepless night, while Father sang a lullaby at the top of his lungs, Mother added up the clues of my unflagging interest in the story of Sergio Ernst which I've been leaving here and there. And no matter how uncomfortable the subject is for her, as far as she can see it's the only way to bring me closer to Father. In her view, rather than listen to my misguided ideas about literature, Father will always prefer to hear my brother tell him the latest antics of Little Lulu or provide news of Brigitte Bardot. But I might be able to get his attention, win a few points, make him truly see me, if I succeed in locating a child of uncertain identity, who perhaps survived the years of horror in a city that was bombed and split in half. Because even if Father learns all languages and devours every library in the world, he might not be able to finish his *magnum opus* until he fills this little gap in his own knowledge. Ergo, this morning, Mother called me into her room under the pretext of asking me to get St Augustine's *Confessions* down from the top shelf for her. She asked me to remove my shoes so I could climb on the night-stand, and that was when I saw her drawer of secrets ajar for the first time. Then she told me she was going to church, as if I didn't know her Sunday routine, and off she went, leaving the St Augustine on the bed.

With this new information in hand, I was going to consider my next moves, but Mother expedited matters when she saddled me with the Beauregards' little por-celain plate with a slice of pineapple pie on it. She insisted I deliver it before lunch and thank my German friend for her. She was afraid it would lose its sheen, but the thing stuck to the plate in my hands is a discoloured blob with a half-circle of rust-coloured pineapple on top. I take a detour to the neighbourhood of Santa Cecília, where there's a Portuguese cake shop open on Sundays, and replace the pie with half a dozen custard tarts. It's a sultry day, with heavy clouds, and from the Beauregards' gate I believe I hear Henri having a temper tantrum behind the ever-shuttered windows. But when Madame Beauregard opens the door before I even ring the bell, I realize that her husband's bellowing is just a long-distance phone call in German: I'll send you the Ravel scores by express post, with my regards to Maestro Köll-reuter! When she sees me, Madame just about locks herself in the house again, having noted, no doubt, the sorry impression she's made on me, and not just because she is in a dressing gown with no make-up on her sleepy face. Doubtless, she now understands that she has just been demoted from the role of woman loved and possessed by Father; she who I secretly desired as one might a desirable mother. I think she knew all along that I'd taken her for someone else, and took a coquettish pleasure in passing herself off as another woman, if for no other reason than to practise the dramatic art she learned in her youth. Schooled in the Stanislavski method, she was beginning to feel at home in the character of Anne Ernst, whose husband she stole in real life. And now a cloud of hostility descends between us: Oh, no, here again, Monsieur? She retrieves the watering can from a corner of the patio, turns on a tap and takes out her irritation on the cat with a squirt of water. I only came to bring you some custard tarts, Madame, one of my mother's specialities. Oh, *merci*, how kind of your mother, wanting me to become a whale with her Portuguese sweets. And, watering the geraniums: You can put them on the wall there. Henri has the stomach of a goat, he'll eat anything. Incidentally, Madame Beauregard, I was intrigued to hear your husband just now. I was under the impression that you didn't like Germans. Madame turns to me brandishing the watering can: Henri was born in Berlin but he isn't German, Monsieur Hollander. He is as much a French citizen as I am and holds that country in contempt, even more so than I do. At this, annoyed by her tone of voice and exasperated with Henri's interminable piano exercise, I blurt out: I want to speak to the maestro, it's a matter that concerns him. Deaf to my demand, she squats to pick a sickly flower, but can't resist taking a peek at the photograph I hold up: This is my brother Sergio with his mother Anne Ernst, a Berliner whom the prominent pianist Heinz Borgart knew very well. I was going to show her Anne's letter, too, but Madame is truly intractable today: Henri may have had his way with I-don't-care-how-many Annes when he was single, Monsieur, but not with that one there, who looks more like a chambermaid. Michelle! calls her husband, and she leaves the watering can capsized on the ground: *Adieu*, Monsieur, I wish you a safe journey. And when she sees the first few drops of rain plop onto the geraniums she has just watered, she mutters: *Merde.* It rains on the custard tarts, the cat meows on the doormat, and I am debating whether to leave or stay when the door opens again. It's Christian in a suit and tie, holding an umbrella, to whom I promptly extend my hand: Good morning, Christian, do you know where Rua Teodoro Sampaio is? Not only does he allow me to accompany him but he also offers me half of his umbrella, an amiability I find touching: *Danke, Sie sind zu liebenswürdig!* What, you don't speak German? Your father didn't teach you? I am a great admirer of Heinz Borgart, his recordings of Schubert are always on my gramophone. What, you're not familiar with them? You don't like music? Ah, I appreciate French literature too. Russian literature? You don't say, I'm reading *The Brothers Karamazov* for the seventh time. A French edition, of course, they're the best translations. What, you read them in the original? In the Cyrillic alphabet? My, not even Father speaks Russian. Which bus are we waiting for? Taxi? You don't say, me too.

Christian gives the driver the address of the Hotel

Danúbio, where his girlfriend is staying, coincidentally located next to a German restaurant where it wouldn't be a bad idea to grab some lunch shortly. He doesn't know the Zillertal, unlike his father, who says he hates Germany but can't live without his beer-braised pork knuckles. I invite him and his girlfriend to lunch; they serve *feijoada* at the weekend. But his girlfriend doesn't want to leave her room. She arrived in São Paulo this morning and flies out early tomorrow. An air hostess's life is complicated. It messes with her sleep, her bowels, her menstrual cycle. But for a boyfriend it's not too bad. At the end of the year Christian will be entitled to an Air France ticket to Paris. He has already discovered that there will be an auction of André Gide's manuscripts in January, and he is saving up to make a bid. A postcard from the Congo with a succinct message and Gide's signature can be bought for under 800 francs, a steal. Born in São Paulo, Christian Beauregard is a teacher at the Alliance Française, knows almost as much as I do about French authors, and throughout our conversation we transition from French to Portuguese and back again without realizing it. I think it is in French that we say goodbye at the door of the Danúbio, and a hundred metres further along I get out of the taxi in the fine rain, with the feeling that today saw the beginning of a friendship. Let's hope it is enduring, full of long conversations in which we switch seamlessly between languages at the slightest hint of a misunderstanding. Which reminds me, conversely, of Ariosto, who always talked shit and was pig-headed: he had fixed ideas in just one language. It is true that in his Cassius Clay phase he took to speaking a little English, and even learned some American slang I'd never heard before. To encourage him, I gave him a Jack Kerouac as a gift, thinking he might like him. But Ariosto had no patience for reading and got fed up after the first few pages. He thought the guy's English was crap. And he went about talking to himself in an English of his own invention, an intricate language composed entirely of misconstructions. More recently we couldn't even communicate in Portuguese; his cryptic vocabulary disturbed me. I no longer went out drinking with Ariosto, for fear that at some point he would let slip his new codenames, or push me to join the cause of God-knows-what acronym. I confess that these days, when entering or leaving the house, I always double around the block to avoid passing in front of his place. And I've stopped responding to the two-part whistle he taught me when we were children, the one Zorro used to call Tornado. The same whistle that seems to come out of nowhere from time to time, in the classroom, in a cafe, in the cinema, and which at this very instant finds me on the edge of a kerb, where, with barely contained impulses, I am staring at the wheels of cars tearing past at eighty kilometres an hour. The lights are unchanging, the cars unceasing, and to kill time I browse the newspapers on a newsstand. On a very inky first page with more pictures than text, I read that a guerrilla was killed in a confrontation with police in São Paulo, in the neighbourhood of Consolação. Then my eyes flit to a picture of last night's football match, to someone being arrested during a cocaine bust, to a close-up of a rapist, and then, without meaning to, I return to the story about the guerrilla killed in a confrontation with police in São

Paulo, yesterday at 12.30 p.m., in the neighbourhood of Consolação. I close my eyes, so as not to see his remains, but when I reopen them the picture I'm looking at is of a racing-car driver decapitated in a collision in Indianapolis, then without meaning to I return to the story about the guerrilla killed after a bloody shoot-out with police in São Paulo, yesterday at 12.30 p.m., on Rua Gravataí, in the neighbourhood of Consolação. The two-part whistle I've just heard has come from a traffic cop, and when I see the flow of pedestrians over the zebra crossing I sprint to the other side of the road. With my heart pounding, I take a deep breath and glance around, except now I can't remember why I wanted to cross the street so badly. This side is like a mirror of the first, with the same pedestrians anxious to cross back over, the same tiny watering holes with their patrons' backsides facing the street, along with an identikit newsstand, where I spot a grisly front page with news of a bloody shoot-out, yesterday at 12.30 p.m., in the vicinity of a day-care centre and a boarding house, on Rua Gravataí, Consolação. But the name of the dead guerrilla isn't Ariosto Fortunato, as I thought for a split second; rather, it is Akihiko Matsumoto, aka 'The Japanese'.

12

I've known Eleonora Fortunato since I was a child,
although she rarely came down from her studio in the
attic. Sometimes, when I saw her going past, I thought
she was Captain Marvel's father, as no one else in the
house wore trousers. Later the fashion caught on among
other women, but to me, trousers made their legs look
short, compared to Eleonora Fortunato's. She also had a
long neck, as spindly legged birds do, and her triangular
face, even when made up to go out, had a somewhat
masculine beauty about it. I can barely remember her
voice, much less a smile, as she had no time for children,
and even as an adult I don't think she ever looked in my
direction. Hence my surprise when I find her waiting
for me early one morning, with dark circles under her
bloodshot eyes and her long grey hair in disarray, as if a
few locks were missing. When I enter the sitting room,
Mother is pouring her a straight whisky and shaking her
head emphatically, because Eleonora Fortunato has just
asked in a deep voice if, by any chance, she looks like a
cow. Unable to hold it in, she asks if it isn't rich when
the father of your child, busy with his herds in Mato
Grosso, doesn't deign to reply to a desperate telegram.
And when she sees me she adds in the same tone: And

you, can you believe that not even my lawyer will talk to me? They're a bunch of wimps, she says, they're a bunch of fucking wimps, and her voice grows louder and louder, perhaps with the intention of being heard upstairs in Father's study. Getting to her feet, she declares that she won a silver medal in the Belas Artes Exhibition, was featured in the last São Paulo Biennial, used to give interviews about abstract art on a weekly basis, and now she can't even get the newspapers to print a few lines. You're a fucking wimp too, she spits at me, citing, however, what she spat at the Military Police commander, who doesn't have the balls to confront the agents who made her son disappear. The lying prick showed her some files with terrifying pictures of burglars, drug dealers and murderers, when everyone knew Ariosto wasn't a dangerous felon but a kid from a good family with shit for brains. After a week without any news, Eleonora Fortunato says the only thing left for her to do was to go to Reichel, an industrialist who, according to gossip in high circles, has friends in the military. She already knew him from vernissages and had sold him a painting years earlier, so she was furious when she was barred entry to his mansion. She cursed the guard, quarrelled with the dogs, and kicked up such a stink that Reichel's wife came to see her in the garden, but as she walked out of the door she was already calling Eleonora a cow, and worse. Eleonora tried to appeal to Mrs Reichel's maternal sentiment, given that she is a mother too, and received as a response: But no son of mine is a son of a bitch. And this is where I come in. Eleonora Fortunato wants me to talk to Udo. She believes Udo Reichel will talk to his father if he's told that his best friend was dragged out of the house by plain-clothes police officers, never to be seen again. I promise to do as she asks. I can hardly tell a woman in such a state that I barely know Udo and don't even know where he lives. I certainly can't tell her that I doubt Udo would be willing to help the person who slashed his face with a shard of glass. And no sooner has she left than Father starts talking loudly and confusedly in the study. Troglodytes, I think I hear, they're monoglot shites, and I more or less understand that he is talking about the Ariosto Fortunato case. Bunch of torturers, I hear loud and clear now, and although his indignation is more than justified, Father should really be more careful about what he says over the phone. It's because you're a wimp, he shouts, you won't publish it because you're a fucking wimp! And with these words, Father, who has just retired from public service, puts an end to his long collaboration with *A Gazeta*.

I am late for work, find my classroom empty, and in the front office I am told that the director wants to talk to me in private. Natércia and I go way back. We took this very same prep course together, and in the university entrance exam, which I coasted through, she placed first. Just out of university, where she was top of the class, she took over as director of the prep course and invited me to teach Portuguese. Every so often she'd call me into her office, and it pleased me to see that the country girl, who'd been so bashful when I met her, a real hick, was now a talkative, assertive version of herself, always in stilettos or leather boots. Our conversations about surrealist poets would stretch on into the afternoon, and from work we'd head out for a drink, or to catch a play, and it wasn't uncommon for us to end up in my bed. But after she got married Natércia started to avoid me, and when she summons me to her office this morning it is for me to sign two copies of my letter of resignation. For strictly personal reasons, says the letter, closing a chapter in my life, seeking new challenges, professional growth, etc. There has been a complaint that she really should investigate, and if it were any other employee she wouldn't hesitate to open an inquiry. But out of consideration for our old ties, she is giving me the opportunity to leave the job discreetly and of my own volition. I look into her yellow eyes, trying to guess what cards she has up her sleeve, and am inclined to call her bluff, but she glares back at me and doesn't look like she is kidding. I decide it isn't worth grovelling for a pitiful salary, sign the papers in which I give up any claims to compensation of any description and leave the room without saying goodbye to that nymphomaniac. I stop by the front office to get my belongings and note that everyone there already knows of my disgrace; even in the cleaning lady's cross-eyed gaze I see that I am a *persona non grata*. And wandering through the city, I speculate about the real reason for my dismissal, beginning with the understandable jealousy of Natércia's husband, an elderly man, dean of the Law department. On the other hand, it could be that this ambitious woman, who obtained her PhD in Language and Literature not so long ago, who was testing my patience in bed with questions of semiotics just the other day, sees me as competition now that the chair of Comparative Literature is up for grabs, seeing as how its occupant has gone into exile in Chile.

I can't dismiss the possibility, either, that she encouraged students to file complaints about me, whether for perpetual tardiness, too many no-shows, alcohol on my breath, or even possession of LSD. But the most serious thing, in the current climate, is that quitting in dubious circumstances creates the suspicion that I am something of a lefty, while Natércia, like all swots, has never gone anywhere near the student movement. And if the current chancellor's office decides to look into my background, my proximity to opponents of the regime, or even urban guerrillas, will necessarily come to light. My name will quickly find its way onto a blacklist and state schools will close their doors to me; I won't even be welcome in Catholic schools. Then I remember Christian. I doubt the agents of repression would dare go snooping around the Alliance Française. With a job at the Alliance, no matter how inconsequential, I'll be able to apply myself to my research far from the intrigues of academic circles, while waiting for the wind to change in the country. Besides which, working alongside Christian on a day-to-day basis, I won't want for opportunities to exchange a few words with Heinz Borgart, in spite of his wife. So I head to the school in the city centre, confident in my university-level French, which in practice is even more fluent than my friend's. When I get there, though, I flaunt my skills in vain, because the receptionist, with her broken French, thinks that I've come to enrol and recommends the excellent night classes for adults. I ask to speak to her superior, but she says Madame Nicole has just nipped out to a doctor's appointment. She had to pay her gynaecologist an urgent visit after a little spotting. As for Christian

Beauregard, he is her favourite teacher, perhaps because he's a Sagittarian like her, but he's giving a class at the moment and nothing in the world could convince her to call him out of class for a minute. At any rate, if I decide to wait, there's a waiting room with a sofa and a pile of magazines on a coffee table. She also shows me the toilet, a drinking fountain, mentions that she heard on the radio that it was 38°C in the shade and nibbles at a bar of chocolate: Want some? I leaf through three or four issues of *Paris Match* then try the receptionist for something else to occupy myself with, but all she has to offer me is her photo novel. There must be some books in the director's office, but she isn't authorized to remove them from there. After much reluctance, however, she ends up bringing me, for a quick look, what she finds in Madame Nicole's drawer. It is a pocket edition of *Justine, Les Malheurs de la Vertu*, by the Marquis de Sade: *Yes, Constance, it is to you that I am dedicating this work . . .* Some time ago I held in my hands a limited edition of this novel, which Father keeps on the revolving bookcase beside his lounge chair, safe from Mother. I read it in fits and starts, always on high alert, on the rare occasions that Father left the house, just as I am made aware each minute of Madame Nicole's imminent arrival. *At this period crucial to the virtue of the two maidens, they were in one day made bereft of everything . . .* Voraciously, more with my memory than my eyes, I reread the vicissitudes of poor, God-fearing Justine and her older sister Juliette, abandoned to the pleasures of debauchery. And just at the moment when the younger of the two, aged twelve, repels her pastor's lustful moves, I hide the book from the children and adolescents who fill the waiting room until they merrily trade places with the classes that are leaving. When I reopen it, I imagine that it is illustrated with pictures of the very same girls in bloom who have just gone past, possible future students of mine: *'Oh! Monsieur,' I said in tears, throwing myself at the feet of this barbarous man, 'give way a little, I beg you!'* I imagine Madame Nicole is also interrupted in her reading frequently, as indicated by the folded corners of successive pages. Or it could be that the folds mark the passages she finds most interesting, such as this one, in which Justine, still a virgin, is subjugated by the terrible Ironheart, *as soon as I was in the state he wished me to be in, on all fours, which made me look like an animal* . . . And this is when the receptionist takes a phone call and tells me that Madame Nicole won't be returning to work this afternoon, and it's good that she's taking a week off to rest because she never slows down and has already had two miscarriages. And Ironheart once again threatens to take Justine by force, without harm to her virginity: *If you are afraid of getting pregnant, that could not happen in such a way, so your pretty figure will never be ruined. The maidenhead that is so dear to you will be preserved* . . . Absorbed in my reading, I only realize it is night when I see that my packet of cigarettes is empty. Standing in front of me, Christian holds out his: Want a cancer stick?

I don't know why the hell I had to go and invite Christian to dine at this particular restaurant, now that I am unemployed. La Casserole is one of the most expensive restaurants in São Paulo, and Christian, whose air hostess girlfriend must bring him wines from first class, isn't content with a good Brazilian red. Yet the titles he is carrying in a book strap are, at a glance, less sophisticated than I thought: a *Petit Robert* dictionary, a Portuguese–French–Portuguese Larousse, three grammars, an *Asterix* collection and four *The Adventures of Tintin* comic books, in addition to two volumes with hand-made covers. The first of these he shows me under the table as soon as the maître d' has left with our orders. I thought it was another Marquis de Sade, but it is a Russian book, the title of which Christian underlines with his finger: Мистерия-Буфф, that is, *Mystery-Bouff*, from which, obviously, I deduce that Маякóвский is Mayakovsky. And when I see the name of the author of the second book, Гóголь, I can't help myself: GOGOL? With a hand on my arm Christian warns me that most of the city's waiters, doormen and taxi drivers are police informants, to whom merely knowing how to speak Russian may appear compromising. And when in whispers he compares our police state to that of Nazi Germany, I think he's exaggerating a little. But I take the opportunity to bring up Heinz Borgart, who, in Brazil at least, needn't fear a campaign of racial hygiene. Christian wrinkles his brow as if he doesn't understand and, switching from Portuguese to French, says his father was persecuted by the Gestapo due to his connections to anarchist organizations. Of course, I say, and it was in an anarchist cell in Charlottenburg that he met Anne Ernst. Never heard of her? Here she is, the angle of the photograph doesn't do her justice, her body only just recovered from the pregnancy. The baby? The baby is my brother Sergio, at six months of age. But he could have been your adoptive brother, just take a look at this letter. Today you and I would be brothers by marriage, isn't that incredible? Keep the letter, take the photo too, it'd be interesting to show them to your father. What, you aren't on speaking terms? The waiter brings Christian's starter, a fifty-*cruzeiro* foie gras that he savours in silence. Then he tells me he wants to rent his own apartment if he can get the Alliance to adjust his salary for inflation. He sends back his chateaubriand, he likes his rarer, and asks for a taste of my omelette. He says he wouldn't mind a bedsit in a council building; at least noisy neighbours would be more fun than waking up every day to his father's piano. Even when still a babe in arms, he couldn't understand why his father sat there banging on that huge black box for so many hours. But it wasn't long before he found himself enthroned on the cushioned stool of the brown piano, where he learned to read music before his ABCs; it was a piece of cake. From an early age he resigned himself to six hours of practice every morning, and, like a child prodigy, learned to play any score he set eyes on. Nevertheless, his efforts fell short of his father's expectations; Heinz criticized him for always playing very different pieces in the same mechanical way. As a result, before bed, he was subjected to forty minutes of his father showing off with Chopin so Christian would know what it meant to play with feeling. But no matter how impressed he was with Heinz Borgart's face while playing preludes, little Christian was unable to perceive any feeling at all in the sound of a piano that, frankly, to him was little different from a rattle. He kept at his exercises only to please his father, to whom he didn't dare confess that he had never been able to distinguish between the tones of those notes that his eyes read and his fingers played so faithfully. The essence of music was a mystery to Christian, who, when his mother would sing 'La Vie en Rose' to him in the kitchen, only thought it odd that she likes speaking so slowly to him. Michelle became suspicious and took him to see a specialist, who diagnosed him as having severe congenital amusia, otherwise known as complete tone-deafness. These words were like music, so to speak, to the ears of a boy who imagined that from then on he'd have his mornings free to play football with his school friends. But no, Henri refused to believe such quackery. He thought his son was doing it out of spite and, when he saw Christian desperately thumping the keyboard, sentenced him to six hours of daily seclusion in his bedroom. Michelle tried to defend the child, arguing that even a genius like Charles Darwin suffered from the same disorder, and compared her husband to a vain painter who curses his son for having been born blind. But in the end all she could do was keep the boy company. She learned to play button football on the floor in his room, and one day brought him the only book in the house, an old paperback of La Fontaine's fables from when she was a girl. The moral of the story? Paternal punishment yields the most unexpected fruits. Christian developed a fondness for literature, from the classics that his mother used to buy for him at the French bookshop to the latest international releases that his girlfriend brings him from Paris. And after ordering profiteroles for dessert, he apologizes for venting, but his differences with his father have only become more accentuated as an adult. And if he'd known what my intention was when I sought him out, he'd have discouraged me right there in the waiting room of the Alliance Française. Now it is I who apologize for having spoiled his dinner with such a trivial matter, because what I really want is to land a gig at the Alliance, which has a tradition of taking in political dissidents the world over. I was hoping that Christian would promptly offer to help, that he'd promise, for example, to put in a good word for me with Madame Nicole, but he glances at his watch, is surprised to see that it's already after midnight and orders a Napoléon brandy as a nightcap. In the taxi, he talks quietly in French about his hopes for the weekend, when the air hostess is going to bring him some of Nabokov's earlier books in Russian, which she saw in a second-hand book-shop on Saint-Germain. But I don't register the titles he cites, nor do I follow the directions his monologue takes until the end of our journey, when he passionately holds forth about some of Tolstoy's wife's intimate problems. In front of his darkened house, I decline his invitation to come in and I'm not sure if he is offended. Without saying goodbye, he gets out of the taxi with an ungainly jerk of the body, perhaps due to the alcohol, perhaps the weight of the books.

My house is pitch-black too, but as I pass my brother's door I think I hear a woman sobbing. Some time ago, naively, I actually delighted in the signs of his decline. I'd noticed that this consummate hunter of immaculate maidens had begun to allow second-hand females into his room, some even over the age of twenty. And, not in-frequently, no sooner had they entered than they would become angry and leave, slamming the door behind them. But there were also those who gradually calmed down, or even appeared to enjoy whatever went on in there, though not without first whimpering and begging for mercy like poor Justine: *Oh! Monsieur, I have no experience of such things* . . . I began to suspect that my brother, with urges like those of the abominable Ironheart, was intent on initiating these women in deviant practices of which Mother would never have approved. I do not presume, however, to judge his sexual conduct, not least because lately, with my door open a crack, I have eyed these young women up and down so I can approach them if I ever see them in the bars he frequents over near Rádio Tupi. But tonight, after keeping an eye out until late, I go to bed unsuccessful in my surveillance. And I find it odd, because my brother is a celibate at heart; he has never liked sleeping in the company of anyone else. Once satisfied, he sprawls across the bed, talks about other women, tells scatological jokes, points out cockroaches on the bookcases; in short, he always finds a way to rid himself of his guests. And it's only when I am already under the blanket that I realize I've left the door ajar, but it's better this way, as it's easier to keep tabs on what's going on in the house. Pretending to be asleep, I will leap out of bed at the slightest soundto size up the mysterious female visitor, who might be a complete dog, a hag, an all-time low that my brother hides because it could tarnish his reputation. Or, on the contrary, she might be the one who doesn't wish to be seen with him, an elegant woman, way out of his league, a woman from another walk of life, a married woman.

13

I charge after her without any hope of catching up, because we run down the stairs at the same speed, much faster than the stairs, which have become an escalator. And as Maria Helena slows, I too begin to tire, because the descending escalator has quite possibly veered upwards. I don't know exactly when this phenomenon took place, nor do I have anything by which to measure the incline of the escalator, which rolls on, unimpeded, in the middle of the clouds. I only know the escalator is ascending because I can see Maria Helena at the top, and I only know she's at the top because I can see her white knickers under her skirt. And Maria Helena suddenly gets her period; it appears on the white fabric like a red flower bud and quickly blooms, tingeing the entire garment and dripping blood on the steps that now recede beneath my feet. When I reach the end, exhausted, the sun blinds me and I lose sight of Maria Helena; her menses are absorbed by the sand on a beach that can only be Copacabana. It is, without a doubt, the Copacabana that Maria Helena used to tell me about, with its many bikinis and multicoloured sun umbrellas, with the crests of waves like bulls ready to turn to foam as they break. Then the sky clouds over, the colours fade, the sea grows calm and the sand disappears under a crowd of bodies pressed up against one another. The bodies are naked and I feel my way with my feet, afraid I might wake them, but they are cold and stiff and bony, hard to walk on. No sooner have I grown accustomed to my path of skin, than I have to climb piles of grey bodies, of old people, children, horses, dogs and cats, fish that look like rats, rats that look like pigeons, babies, foetuses and mothers with sagging breasts, but no matter what, I must reach the windowless, whitewashed house at the top, which is either a lifeguard station or a cremation chamber. Here I am, and the puddle of fresh blood on the doormat is a good omen, a sign that my Jewish brother is still alive, albeit bleeding on the cement escalator which leads to a room full of Russian books and writing in Cyrillic on the walls around an unmade bed with a bloodstain that fans across the sheet until it becomes a red flag, on which I intend to sleep deeply. But it is impossible, because there are disturbances on the surface of my dream, there are footsteps that transport a woman's sobs, there are howls, there is someone playing a noteless piano that looks more like a typewriter. *A–Crump*, *Crumpet–Haywire*, *Hazard–Omelet*, *Omen–Skein*, *Skeletal–Zyxomma*, I read the spines of dictionaries with sleep-filled eyes. I see my jeans lying on the floor and I have no difficulty recognizing, in the distance, perhaps coming from downstairs in the sitting room, Eleonora Fortunato's voice. I stretch, go to the toilet, come back, scrutinize the silence in my brother's bedroom, Father wrenches another piece of paper from his Remington and I take my time in bed until I'm sure Ariosto's mother has gone. I find Mother in the sitting room pulling shapeless clothes out of a plastic bag. One by one she smoothes out skirts, shirts, white knickers, folds them carefully and places them in a tattered valise. Now she holds up a polka-dot dress and notices me without seeing me: Your friend's *inamorata* is very thin, and she didn't even want any minestrone. When Mother looks at me she observes, as always, that I don't look well. She feels my forehead with the back of her hand and says that Eleonora Fortunato asked after me. Eleonora had brought over the rest of Tricita's clothing and was pleased to hear that the girl was still resting. She accepted a whisky, fretted about her son and seemed impatient to know how my conversation with that boy Udo had gone, but with the time that I would normally leave for work come and gone, she went off to meet a member of the political opposition, a ruthless congressman. She also hoped to have an audience with the archbishop in the afternoon, which is why she would probably miss Tricita, whom she wished a safe journey home to her country. And without me asking her anything, Mother explains that she'd happily have offered the girl a place in the master bed if Father didn't snore so loudly. She also thought she'd have felt more comfortable with me; with any luck I'd have entertained her with tales of my old sidekick from his Captain America days. But I was still out last night when my brother came home and insisted that Tricita take his bed. He could sleep on a bedroll on the floor, but wouldn't hesitate to bed down on the sofa in the sitting room if she didn't feel comfortable sharing a room with a stranger. He only advised against sleeping in my room, because I came home at all hours, sometimes drunk, sometimes in bad company.

And Tricita only agreed to go upstairs with him, according to Mother, because she was afraid of waking up alone in the middle of the night, tormented as she was by the news of her beloved's kidnapping. Besides, she needed to rest after her long bus journey, not to mention the queues, the traffic and lugging her huge backpack around the city on foot. Having returned from visiting her family in Buenos Aires, she had arrived at the address she had in São Paulo unaware of what had happened, and Eleonora Fortunato had barely opened the door to her. She recommended that Tricita spend the night somewhere less vulnerable, such as down the street with the Hollanders, a family above suspicion. I listen to all of this without making a sound, for who am I to second-guess Mother? But if Eleonora Fortunato had waited for me, I'd have asked her straight out if she knew what kind of reprobate the girl would be spending the night with; had she known, she might have had a little sympathy for her son. Or perhaps Eleonora Fortunato thinks that by now Ariosto has been through so many beatings, electric shocks and humiliations that the stigma of being a cuckold might almost come as a relief. Come to think of it, in a recent nightmare, I remember seeing him hoisted up in the air, with his wrists tied behind his back, until he passed out with dislocated shoulders. And when I got lost fleeing through the corridors of this nightmare, I found him on a dungeon floor, hands and feet bound, his torso convulsing as if something was gnawing at his guts, perhaps a rat rammed up his backside. But just now the image that comes to mind is my brother's hand in the half-light slowly moving down Ariosto's girlfriend's back. This is the scene I am picturing as Mother folds the polka-dot dress and says: Son, stop thinking foolish things. Then I hear the coming and going of footsteps upstairs, the opening and closing of bedroom and bathroom doors, and when Tricita appears on the stairs in trousers, all I can think of is the Eleonora Fortunato of my first libidinous dreams, of my nocturnal emissions. It is her lanky body, her angular face and even her elusive gaze, her way of almost ignoring me when Mother introduces me as Ariosto's bosom buddy. But of course Ariosto has not so much as glimpsed in her what is immediately obvious to me. He no doubt thinks he's attracted to Tricita's tomboyish manner, the way she chews gum with her mouth open, wears trainers with scuffed toes and lugs around a camping backpack. A certain awkwardness, that of a girl who has grown up without realizing it, a kind of semi-innocence that is, invariably, irresistible to my brother, who trails after her, fawning over her, a clear indication that he has yet to reach his goal. He invites her to have breakfast, says she smells lovely after her shower, but I think it'll be hard for him to win her over with his apery of Spanish: *Me gustatu hair wetito*. Tricita has other things to do today. She intends to drop off some *regalitos* that Brazilian friends in Buenos Aires sent for loved ones. And Mother, folding one last blouse, asks her to excuse the valise, which is as old as its owner, both having come from Italy before the war. She suggests that one of her sons give their guest a hand with her luggage, but Tricita assures her that the backpack is light, it's mostly just Argentinian biscuits. She is amazed that Mother has never tried *alfajores* and gives her a packet of the Havanna brand: *Son muy ricos, con dulce de leche.* Which is the cue for Father to appear in pyjamas at the top of the stairs: What's this about biscuits? And after pulling out a São Paulo travel guide, Tricita tries to pronounce some addresses she has memorized, in parts of town that my brother, over her shoulder, points to on the map: Santo Amaro, Paraíso, Vila Maria, Bom Retiro, Tatuapé, Freguesia do Ó . . . I offer to guide her on her expedition, given that in an ever-growing São Paulo, no sooner has a map been printed than it becomes obsolete. Not to mention that a young woman on her own will always be prey to sleazebags and delinquents, I say, meaning that not even her backpack will prevent her from being dry-humped on the city's packed buses. Meanwhile, however, my brother has already extorted enough money from Father for a week's worth of taxi rides. Well, I have a better idea: I can deliver the gifts while Tricita goes straight to the bus station. But she insists on delivering the *alfajores* herself, seeing as how she doesn't intend to return to Buenos Aires right away, and surely one of the families she'll be visiting will offer to put her up. She'd rather have her legs cut off than leave Brazil without her beloved, she declares with Hispanic vigour, then bites her bottom lip and lowers her eyes brimming with tears. My brother tells her that it would be an insult to Father, Mother, and him in particular, should she refuse our hospitality. With the tip of his finger he raises her chin towards him and announces: *No problemo, let's vamos in uno taxi.* And when Tricita lets him take off her back-pack, it occurs to me that this is just the first step in her allowing herself to be undressed.

I don't want to be home to hear Argentinian moans coming from my brother's bed. Nor would I like to be in my room when she knocks on my door with her clothes in disarray. So Christian's phone call to say that Colette, his nickname for Nicole, asked me to stop by the Alliance Française in the early evening couldn't have come at a better time. Dressed in a suit and tie, before leaving I go to the shelf of French poets, the same ones I lent Maria Helena years ago, poets who I read differently each time I return to them, trying to imagine on occasion how she might have read them. I think I already read Rimbaud with a woman's eyes, and any one of his poems will be good company for me in the waiting room, in addition to making me look good to Colette. But Madame Nicole can't see me after all, she's in a meeting with her ex-husband, who in the receptionist's opinion is the spitting image of Elizabeth Taylor's ex. If it's true that he beats her, not Richard Burton but the ex, that's Madame Nicole's business; she told the receptionist to wish me good luck and give me a leaflet with the requirements and dates of the admission exam for Alliance teachers at provincial branches. There is mayhem and hoots of laughter as herds of students jostle past me and spill into the street. Right behind them is Christian, who looks surprised to see me, smiles, and rests his bundle of books on the receptionist's desk. I thought he was going to shake my hand, but it is Rimbaud that he picks up, astounded to see a 1920 edition of *Le Bateau Ivre*, illustrated with two sketches by the poet himself. He examines the little book, estimates that it's worth a fortune, and on his way out suggests we dine at La Cocagne, much better than last night's restaurant. He is about to wave down a taxi when I tell him that I came unprepared, I don't have my wallet on me, only a little loose change. On the bus, he takes the last free seat and reads the poem five times in a row before we get off at the corner by his house. I try to make conversation and thank him for putting in a good word for me with Colette, but he walks quickly in front of me. So I tell him I've decided I don't want a job at the Alliance any more, now that the publisher has approved my manuscript and made me an offer with an advance and everything. A novel, yep, a *roman à clef*, I can't believe I've never told you about it. The publisher? Privilégio, Editora Privilégio, a small house, not very well known, but open to new talent. Heinz Borgart's piano can already be heard when Christian comes to a halt on the pavement, bums a cigarette, and I notice his right eyelid twitching. I knew it, I knew he had literary aspirations, he has a book ready to go in a drawer: But it's poetry and not even Rimbaud made a living from poetry. He says he'd feel a bit embarrassed about taking up an editor's time with some verses he hasn't even had the courage to show his girlfriend. But, anyhow, they're poems along the lines of Yevtushenko and other contemporary Russians, with whom I pretend to be familiar: *The books we read read us too / The books see hidden screams and whispers in our eyes / The books hear all our fears . . .* To my unschooled ears the sentimental piano melody coming from Christian's house and accompanying his recital is Tchaikovsky: *The silent return of borrowed books / By those who love one another / It doesn't seem like a reciprocal favour . . .* With his thinning hair aflap, he is exactly how I'd imagine a Russian poet declaiming in the wind. I feel a sudden rush of admiration for Christian, real pride even, which quickly evaporates, since I can't bear the idea that he, and not I, should publish a book. If I had access to a publisher tomorrow, I don't see why I should recommend Christian, if I might try my hand at literature myself. And just as Christian feels that he can emulate Russian poets, I am surely capable of writing a novel inspired by 1930s Germany, so present in my reading and fantasies. I could write, for example, the story of Anne Ernst, whose photograph with my brother in her arms I keep in my shirt pocket and am compelled to look at several times a day. And I am always getting a fright because it's never where I left it. It's in the right pocket of my jeans, then it ends up, I don't know how, in a back pocket, it vanishes then slips out of my sleeve like a magician's card, and all of a sudden it looks like a Virgin of Hearts with Baby Jesus, and I wonder if Miss Ernst hasn't become a mischievous ghost. Just now the photograph has slipped into my underwear and is stuck to my pubes, and every time I find it again I want to kiss it in thanks. It's hard to believe that this Anne gazing at her child devotedly is the kind of woman who could abandon him at an orphanage. But perhaps what I fail to comprehend today will become clear by the end of the book, when I review what my hand has written unconsciously: *The snow, the snow, the snow, the snow . . . My neighbour came over for a coffee and once again she asked me if my Brazilian lover was the son of savage Indians. When the squall had passed, I dressed the baby to go out and Ingeborg thought he looked*

like an Eskimo . . . I stopped off at two more bookshops on
Kurfürstendamm. I'd accept a job at the till, but I'd rather
go back to being a sales assistant . . . On the first day of
spring I took my son out in the pram for a walk in the
Tiergarten. Ingeborg and her husband, both unemployed
like me, came too. The Schneiders can't even afford coffee,
so I shouldn't complain . . . I finally went to Alexanderplatz
and sold the white-gold ring that S. gave me to Mr Abra-
hamovsky . . . At the edge of the lake Ingeborg asked me if
it was hurtful to be pointed at in the street for being a
single mother. I laughed out loud, really loud, the way S.
liked . . . This morning someone pointed at me in the street
and muttered: Jüdin . . . And here at last is a hypothesis
that has only occurred to me in my worst nightmares,
that Anne Ernst herself had some Jewish blood. And in
this light I can understand how, guided by a premonitory
instinct, in May 1932 she entrusts Sergio Ernst to the
State, requesting that the child's biological father, Sergio
de Hollander, Christian, Brazilian but white-skinned, of
pure Flemish descent, be informed of the fact. He won't
let her down; he will offer to pay the child's travel
expenses and give him a home in Rio de Janeiro. But,
as required by law, Miss Ernst will be granted time to
reflect and, God willing, change her mind about giving
up her child. She still has some time left when the Nazis
come to power, and before the authorities can certify
her identity, and that of her mother and grandmother,
Anne will leave Berlin, disembark in Hamburg, vanish
in Frankfurt to be resurrected in Munich, or perhaps
Vienna. I still don't know if she'll be detained without
papers at a border, if she'll pass herself off as the Kaiser's

granddaughter, if she'll end her days in an asylum or a camp in Poland, but at least she'll always have the consolation of knowing that the child is in good hands, on a sunny beach in Brazil. Though, in fact, he won't be, either because a neighbour informed the authorities of Anne's Jewish origins, because the new German attaché cut off contact with my father, or because Father lost the letter from the consulate inside goodness knows what book. Father could solve this mystery for me if he were open to having a one-on-one conversation. Which wouldn't be entirely unfeasible if he knew I'd become a man of letters. He wouldn't hear about my novel from me, much less the plot I have in mind, even if the real characters' names have been changed or they're referred to by their initials. But I can't stop him receiving a complimentary copy from the publisher, opening it in disbelief, starting to read it reluctantly, and getting caught up against his will in the narrative, which reminds him of episodes lost in memory, perhaps a German book that Assunta won't be able to find on the bookshelves. Nor can I stop Father becoming unusually flustered, because his memory for literature has always been sharper than that of his own existence, and he may not have enough time left in which to reread his entire library. And then he will call me to his study and cough twice and ask me in a threatening tone of voice that breaks into a pleading falsetto the title of the book from which I copied mine. And I will laugh out loud, point to my head and say: From my own *Mangokopf*, based on a true story that I've been researching for years. And my answer will strike him as flawlessly logical, because it came out of my mouth in immaculate German. And from then on we shall communicate only in German, to the chagrin of my brother and the suspicion of my mother, who, without understanding a word, will see her husband forget the food on his plate and say how fascinating he found the young A.E., so much so that S.H. leaving her in Berlin seems most unlikely. And he will confess that he was somewhat frustrated at the end because he wanted to know what happened to the boy. And in the end I will challenge him to reveal what he would have happen to S.E. if he were the writer. But then perhaps he will trail off, stop speaking in German, turn his back on me and ask my brother what he thinks of Argentinian women, and praise Mother's spaghetti alla puttanesca. And Mother will be counting the minutes until dinner is over, when she can shelve my book between the novels of João, Mário, Graciliano and other friends of Father's, intuiting that she will be prouder of me if she doesn't read my work. But she won't be able to stop herself from taking a quick peek and, opening the book at random, her eyes will, unfortunately, fall on a sex scene. At least this time it won't be a sixty-niner or anything similar involving Father, but austere intercourse between A.E. and H.B., a pianist who deserves a chapter all of his own. A pianist who Miss E. believed willing to take her and her son on tour in America, before discovering that she was just another A. with whom he'd had his way. This same pianist from whom I am now separated only by a shuttered window, who in the course of a talk man-to-man, with plenty of beer, could be encouraged to brag of his philandering days. This old goat, who has just shut the piano and is already on his way to the bathroom, will soon sit down at the dinner table and shortly thereafter go to bed with his wife. But Christian isn't in a hurry, he says that in addition to being a poet he is also a translator and that he has translated directly from Russian the entire poetic *oeuvre* of Pasternak, who in principle he would also like to see published here: *Snow is falling, snow is falling / Not snowflakes stealing down / Sky parachutes to earth instead / in his worn dressing gown . . .* He stops abruptly, says he's just had a brilliant idea, gives me a kind of salute and hurries into the house. My hands feel empty; I pat myself all over and find Anne's photograph in the handkerchief pocket of my suit jacket. But it isn't the photograph I'm missing, it's the Rimbaud that Christian didn't give back. I ring the doorbell several times but no one answers, so I leave, but I don't feel like going home. Surely at the Riviera they'll let me put three or four whiskies on a tab.

14

He must be with the girl in a hotel somewhere, I say to pacify Mother, who was up all night because she had a bad feeling. Still in her nightgown with her hair in disarray, she is heating up milk for my breakfast when someone rings the doorbell insistently. It's him, it can only be Mimmo, who has lost his keys again, but when she opens the door my petite mother is trampled by four intruders who, without introduction, ask if this is the residence of Domingos de Hollander. *Mio figlio! Dov'è mio figlio?* Whenever she is on the verge of tears Mother regresses to her native tongue. They ask if I speak Portuguese, announce a search for our Argentinian guest's belongings, and I have no choice but to show them to the valise containing Tricita's things on the sofa in the sitting room. *La valigia di mia mamma!* protests Mother as she watches them slash the lining of the valise with pocket-knives, after tossing Tricita's knickers, blouses, skirts and polka-dot dress onto the rug. It isn't enough; they're looking for letters, notes, agendas, diaries, Marxist publications, and by now the pandemonium must have reached the study, where Father, always vaguely tuned in, is probably thinking it's more of those youths eager for literature, to whom he never refuses to lend his books.

And when someone mentions the name Beatriz Alessandri, he suggests that Mother look on the Spanish American bookcase, as he vaguely remembers such a character in a short story by Borges. A thickset fellow wants to know which Borges the old boy upstairs is on about, because he is Borges, as he shows me in his wallet: *Jorge Borges – Police Inspector*. I try to joke about the coincidence, point to the top of the bookcase, which is out of my reach, and promise him a copy of his namesake if there is a duplicate. But the inspector isn't in a joking mood; he signals for the three gorillas to evacuate the shelf of Argentinian fiction writers and a first edition of *El Aleph*, its spine reinforced with plasters, winds up in his hands. With a stubby, dirty-nailed thumb, he flicks through the book back to front as if it were a stack of playing cards, and between the cover and the title page he finds a note, which I insist on translating for him. It's a few lines from the editor Gonzalo Losada, vigorously recommending Borges's short stories to Father. I point out to him that it dates from 1949, but he isn't interested in stories and orders his henchmen to confiscate the book, which they throw in a canvas bag, oblivious to Mother's indignation. They also discover a piece of paper inside a Cortázar with the following note: *Los pocos lectores que en el mundo había* [illegible] *se pondrán también de escribas*. Borges snorts when he sees Father's scrawl, which to him looks more like a coded message, and impounds the Cortázar also, just in case. I take him aside and explain that this Beatriz Alessandri, whom we know as Tricita, accidentally spent the night at our place, but no one told her to make herself at home with the library.

And, in an effort to impose some limits, I suggest they take a look at the room where she slept, as the pigs are now attacking the shelves of Chileans and Cubans. Disturbed from his reading, Father watches from the door of the study as the four men with oily hair and dandruff-speckled blazers climb the stairs behind me. Who are these quadrupeds? he asks, but fortunately only I understand him, because when Father is upset his diction is worse than his handwriting. His face is inflamed, his cheeks quivering, and Mother ushers him back to the lounge chair, where she takes his blood pressure and gives him a tranquillizer to dissolve under his tongue. In my brother's room, the agents run their eyes over the walls of books and look startled by the task in front of them. They put their hands on top of the books and, with great effort, pull them out in blocks to peer behind them, where they find new walls of books, even more compact, between which cockroaches slip as if through veins in a slab of marble. They soon give up on the bookcases and start rummaging through my brother's desk, on top of which are nothing but porno magazines. The first drawer is full of condoms and Vaseline, but the second is locked, forcing one of the grunts to use a lock pick. And I am shocked to see Borges pull out a sepia photograph of my father with Anne Ernst, which he forgets among the harlots on the magazine covers. At the bottom of this drawer there is also a cardboard file that contains German manuscripts belonging to Father and a document with what looks like the City of Berlin stamp at the top. It's just a bunch of old papers from Germany, I say, offering to translate them, but the inspector, keen to score points with his superiors, or merely wishing to punish my eagerness, decides to confiscate them too. He flings the file into the bag, looks at the bookcases with an air of disgust and wraps up the operation. And after accompanying them to the door, I race back upstairs, afraid I'll find Mother snooping around my brother's room. I now examine at close range the photograph of my lanky father in a bowler hat and bowtie, embracing an Anne Ernst who is already visibly pregnant in her fitted dress, in front of a two-storey house with an alfresco dining area. I imagine it is a literary cafe, because on the back it says in rightward-sloping handwriting: *Sergio und Anne, Literaturhaus, 11-7-30.* Anne's physiognomy isn't anything new to Mother, seeing as how she must be tired of seeing her pictured with the baby in her arms, trying to understand what Father saw in her. But she'd surely be shaken if she saw her looking so radiant, very much her own woman, and Father's too, his son like a king in her belly. I hide the photograph, which Father entrusted to my brother as if in a will, under the raided drawer. And I finally understand who they must have been talking about so much, late into the night, when they sat side by side in the study. Because Father, like me, is incapable of keeping a secret, but, for obvious reasons, he can't very well open up to his friends in artistic circles if he wants to maintain a modicum of discretion about his affair in Berlin. With Mother he avoids stirring up any jealousy of the past; better to let her think he never heard from Anne Ernst again after the wicked woman left the child in the care of the State. But the explanation he may have demanded from Anne, the answers he did or didn't get, the letters he sent to the German authorities, the truth about what happened to Sergio Ernst, which I've been investigating so doggedly, all this he appears to have offered up on a plate to my brother, who probably had little idea where Germany was and would never learn to pronounce Ernst. And Father would have urged him to lock this collection of papers in a drawer, which in all likelihood my brother never opened again because he'd lost the key. And now they are in the possession of the police, to be pored over by a detective who barely understands German, and finally dispatched for filing in an inactive archive.

Assunta! Assunta! Assunta, where's the *Orlando*? Mother would turn down the stove, leave the pasta in the water, ask the young ladies to excuse her, fetch the *Orlando*, or the *Ulysses*, or the *Lady Chatterley*, or Sophocles' tragedies, take them up to the study and return to the kitchen panting, and the scene would repeat itself night after night. And every evening the cast of women in the sitting room grew, offering a kind of retrospective of my brother's love life. They brought jugs of wine to go with the spaghetti and there was always a guitar to lead songs by Violeta Parra and Joan Baez. Sitting on the floor, they whispered, snivelled and laughed quietly, but as soon as I came home they would lower their eyes, as my presence made my brother's absence more painful, if not intolerable. I was like a negative of him, even to Eleonora Fortunato, who ignored me as she handed out T-shirts with the face of her missing son on them. Mother wasn't keen on the T-shirts; she thought they were bad luck and was afraid the exes would ask the painter to make them ones with Mimmo's face on them. But to Eleonora Fortunato my brother was small fry; after being slapped around a bit down at the police station, he would come swaggering back, handsome as ever. She compared him to Assunta's valise: a good seamstress would have it looking brand new in no time, unlike the paintings and etchings that the police had hacked to shreds with pocketknives the last time they raided her house. She added that my brother had an illustrious, well-connected father, rather than a screwball mother like her. This was true and Father did in fact appeal to the São Paulo secretary of justice, who called him back promptly to say he hadn't managed to locate the boy in any of the state's facilities. Even the editor of *A Gazeta*, with whom Father had broken off ties, was helpful and confirmed that the newspaper hadn't registered any traffic accident, bar brawl or police incident involving Domingos de Hollander in the last few days. Then Mother got it into her head that her son had skipped off to Buenos Aires with Tricita. As a matter of fact, she had predicted something of the sort the first time they met, when the air had filled with an electricity that took her back to the night she met my father at a carnival parade. And when she saw Father looking more and more miserable, she tried to persuade him that soon someone would come bearing letters and photographs of the couple, along with packets of *alfajores*. Mother told my brother's ex-girlfriends how delightful her Argentinian daughter-in-law was, how hard she had prayed for her son to marry a decent girl. She also thought it proper to thank Eleonora Fortunato for having sent her the girl, who, God willing, would give her a grandchild the following year. And because no one dared contradict Mother, the vigil cooled and the visits ended in a week. I was the only one left to feed Mother's fantasies, to conjure up the betrothed in Buenos Aires, now drinking hot chocolate in the Café Tortoni, now strolling through Plaza San Martín, now greeting a blind poet on Calle Maipú. I was almost beginning to believe the things I made up, and even found myself nurturing a certain esteem for my fictitious brother and his unfaithful *muchacha*. At the same time it angered me to imagine poor, dishonoured Ariosto's face should we ever meet again, which Christian thought was out of the question. In his opinion, with all due respect to my childhood friend, all armed struggle in South America was just suicidal bravado. Without wanting to sound pessimistic, Christian said he wouldn't like to be in my brother's shoes either, if indeed he had been intercepted with that *guerrillera* and her backpack full of clandestine messages. And I, who had never been crazy about that Brazilian brother, I, who would have exchanged him for a German brother without a second thought, began to feel nervous about being left with no brother at all.

In those days of uncertainty Mother and I would both give a start every time the doorbell rang. While I feared news of a death, she longed for a letter, a postcard, a telegram from Argentina. But, naturally, after a time without any news, I grew indifferent to the doorbell, as one who lives behind a cathedral must become deaf to the bells. Every morning the postman would bring books and more books in packages that Mother didn't even open any more, letting them pile up on the sitting-room floor. There was no point in taking them to Father, who now spent all of his time reclining on his lounge chair, his eyes blank, a closed Proust on his lap and the butt of a Gauloises between his fingers. He refused to go to bed, barely touched the food Mother brought him and only got up to go to the toilet, leaning on Mother. Dr Zuzarte had already examined him and wanted to have him admitted so he could have some X-rays done, but Father dreaded hospitals. So Mother dragged my brother's bedroll into the study, where she would lie at her husband's feet each night, without sleeping a wink. And so that I could respond in an emergency, I began to sleep in my brother's bedroom next door with the door open. Because I'd only ever snuck into his room to fetch an Unamuno or return a Lorca, I'd never even sat on his bed before. And now I was developing a taste for the softness of his mattress, for his sheets, which no matter how many times they'd been washed, never lost their smell of women. When I woke up, I helped myself to his wardrobe, rolling up the legs of his Lee jeans and the sleeves of his linen shirts, which hung down to my thighs like tunics. It is possible that Father mistook me for my brother when he saw me in those clothes, because he'd become agitated, look like he was about to say something, wheeze, wheeze, then cough. And one day when Mother went out to Mass, it occurred to me to show Father the photograph of him with Anne at the literary cafe, to stir up some fond memories. I sat on the chair beside him for the first time, leaned over the lounge chair and even dared sing the waltz from *The Blue Angel* the way he did, while I made the photograph dance here and there, in circles, in a zigzag, thinking his eyes would follow it. But he kept them trained on me, frightened eyes that suddenly reminded me of the expression of little Sergio Ernst in his mother's arms.

It was no novelty for Mother to pray a novena to San Gennaro for Father, hoping he still might recover his faith. And in the last few days she's been trying to convince me that, with his laborious death rattles, he is showing repentance for the sins he committed during his life, of which there are many. From what I know of Father, neither his knowledge of the Holy Scriptures nor his meticulous reading of the *Summa Theologiæ* have made him any less of an atheist. I can understand, however, that finding himself at the door of hell, which in his nightmares is, perhaps, an eternity without books, or an infinite bookshop with its titles in embers, he might have crumbled. It could also be that he has only agreed to the sacrament tonight to make Mother happy one last time. At any rate, whether he wants to or not, he no longer has the strength to boot out old Vicar Bonnet, who arrives with his holy oils for the last rites. And when he sees the priest's white whiskers at close range, Father's voice crackles: St Jerome . . . He is delirious, of course, but the fact that he has spoken in these circumstances, after so many days of silence, feels like a miracle. My son, says the priest, I am Vicar Bonnet and I have come from the Igreja do Calvário to administer the anointing of the sick. But Father insists: St Jerome . . . St Jerome, where's Assunta? And Mother, taking his hand, says: I'm here, Sergio, shall I fetch St Jerome from the bookcase? Father squeezes her hand, falls silent, and the priest begins: Through this Holy Unction and through the great goodness of His mercy, the Lord pardons you . . . The doorbell rings and I answer it apprehensively, because the postman doesn't come at this hour. It's a private chauffeur who hands me a package of books and a note from the Secretary of Justice apologizing for the misunderstanding. I discard the Borges, the Cortázar, the Nerudas and the two volumes of Nicolás Guillén's poetry to get to the cardboard file at the bottom of the package. But it is missing the City of Berlin letterheaded paper which I remember seeing in the inspector's hands. I can, however, work out its likely content from the three incomplete drafts of letters, in my father's handwriting, which I translate as follows:

Rio, 15 December 1936

Municipal Welfare Officer
Berlin City Council

Dear Sir!
    Since I received your letter of 15 May 1936, I have gone to great lengths to gather all of the documents required for Sergio Ernst's adoption in Germany. As I explained previously, Brazilian birth certificates make no mention of religion and hence won't satisfy the German court's requirements.
    I mentioned to you the possibility of obtaining my forebears' baptism certificates. Because Catholicism was the religion of Brazil until 1889, baptism certificates were, in fact, the only birth certificates that existed back then. It is very hard, however, almost impossible, to obtain such documents, as one would

have to know for certain where they are (city and church) in advance. In my case, this investigation is even more difficult because my grandparents came from several

Rio, November 1937

To the Deputy Mayor
of the Regional Administration of Tiergarten, Berlin
Secretariat for Childhood and Youth, Child Welfare

Since my reply to your letter of 26 May 1937, I did my best to obtain all of the required certificates, mine and my relatives', in order to prove the Aryan origin of the child Sergio Ernst, who is in State care. Unfortunately, conditions here in Brazil don't make such investigations easy. There weren't even birth certificates prior to 1889, because Catholicism was our state religion until then, and the only certificates were

So far, I only have my baptism certificate, my mother's baptism certificate and my parents' marriage certificate. I haven't been able to obtain my father's baptism certificate. I have written without success to Pernambuco – the state where my father was born, far from Rio. They weren't even able to tell me the church where my late father was baptized.

Can I not send a monthly stipend to support the child? Now that he is going to turn seven, I renew my suggestion and ask that you be so kind as to convey it to Miss Ernst. I would be eternally grateful if you could do this for me. If Sergio Ernst could come here, it would give me great pleasure to provide him with a good education. If this isn't possible, then who should I

Please find enclosed, my mother's and my birth certificates and my parents' marriage certificate.

Rio de Janeiro,

Dear Sir,

Since your last letter, I have searched a number of times

My efforts, however, have yielded no results. I have received no replies to the letters in which I requested

An
Den Bezirksbürgermeister
der Verwaltungsbezirks Tiergarten
Wohlfahrts- und Jugendamt
Abt. Amtsvormundschaft

Rio de Janeiro, XI/37

Sehr geehrter Herr

Seit meiner Antwort an Ihren
Brief vom 26.5.1937 habe ich mir viel
Bemühungen gegeben alle notwendige
Personenstandsurkunden für mich und
meine Vorfahren zum Nachweis der
arischen Abstammung des Kindes Sergio
Ernst unter Amtsvormundschaftstehend
zu beschaffen. Leider erleichtern nicht
die Verhältnisse hier in Brasilien solche
Untersuchungen. Man hatte sogar keine
ämtliche Geburtsurkunde bei uns
bis um 1889 weil der Katholizismus
bis dahin unsere Staatsreligion war,
und so waren die einzige Urkunde
vorhanden die Taufscheine.

15

'Alu?'

'Michelle? Pardon, Madame Beauregard?'

She doesn't answer me or hang up; she seems to have left the phone off the hook. Cutlery clinking on plates, bread being cut with a serrated knife, someone banging a clogged salt shaker against the table; I hear the dinner sounds of a family with nothing to talk about, except for the cat, who won't stop meowing. I stuff the letters in my pocket when I see Mother come down the stairs with the priest, kiss his hand, open the door for him, and head back up to Father, while I continue to hang on the phone waiting for Christian. I wonder about Mother's feelings towards Sergio Ernst, who, as far as she knew, lived with an adoptive family from an early age. She doubt-less always remembered the little German in her prayers, asking that he grow up healthy, not have a complex about not being a real son, and never come to claim his part of the Hollanders' meagre inheritance. Had Mother become aware of the boy's perilous situation, however, she'd have had it in her to adopt him herself and would have urged Father to go and rescue him from Berlin in the middle of the war. And faced with this young Neapolitan bride who held him in such high esteem, it was understandable that

Father would neglect to tell her of his failure in a far more modest mission here in Brazil. Just now I hear a piano chord, followed by Christian's quick footsteps up the stairs. I hang up the phone, reread the letters, read them from back to front, and wonder if Father, still single, dissatisfied with the results of his queries, didn't personally undertake to trace his forefathers in Pernambuco. And, after much hunting through civil registers and parish records on sugar plantations in ruins, perhaps he actually did unearth the genealogical data he was lacking. But, in that case, for one reason or another, he felt that sending what he'd found to Berlin would be counterproductive. I'd like to talk over these particulars with Christian, who is usually up-front with his opinions on any subject. And on top of that he is the son of a Jew, much as he'd rather not admit it, just as I could be the great-grandson of slaves, or a rabbi from Amsterdam. Perhaps Christian would know what might have become of a child of dubious extraction, at the mercy of Nazi officials. Would he have been forgotten in a depot? Would he have been judged according to the kind of hair he had? Would he have been condemned by the shape of his nose? Could a bored bureaucrat, erring on the side of caution, have signed the fatal warrant? I try Christian again but the line is always busy, and it is already after ten when Mother retires to the study, where Father is snoring rhythmically. I decide to go to the Beauregards' house, which I find more sombre than ever, backlit by the moon. I push open the gate and make my way down the side of the building. There is a light on in the bedroom at the back and before I know it I have unwittingly signalled Christian with Zorro's old whistle. He doesn't whistle back, he probably doesn't know how, but he opens the window, unperturbed by my impromptu visit to his moonlit garden at that hour.

Just as Ariosto rarely had me over to his place, Christian has always been secretive about his room, which no one is allowed to enter: not his mother, the air hostess, or anyone else. It is, as one would expect, stuffy, and smells of his body and nicotine, but the scene isn't very different from what I imagined: a mess of books, even in the corners of the bed with its twisted sheets. After showing me a red Soviet football team jersey with CCCP emblazoned across it in white letters, he retrieves a volume of poetry by Пýшкин, that is, Pushkin, from the floor and makes me sit beside him on the bed, determined, once again, to initiate me in the Russian language. But I came here with the intention of discussing Sergio Ernst with him, and I can't be out too long, given the state Father's in. And when I tell him about my dying father, I choke. I seem to sense that it won't be long until, when she hears my footsteps in the front hallway, Mother will lean over the banister and tell me to come upstairs quickly: *Subito! Subito!* She'll open her bottle-green eyes wide, slightly cross-eyed in a way I've never seen before, and burst into tears: He's dead! *Tuo papà* is dead! She'll cry as she breaks the news to me, perhaps more than if she were receiving it, and will start to pat my face like a blind woman. Then I'll hug her to my chest in silence and kiss her head over and over. She'll be distracted for a few moments as I rock her gently, only to start sobbing again as her own voice breaks: *Tuo papà, figliolo!*

È finito! In the study, Dr Zuzarte and an obese gentle-man will give me their condolences and go back to chatting with their backs to Father. I'll leaf through some books, consider turning the revolving bookcase, try not to face Father in the lounge chair looking almost exactly as he did until just a little while ago, with his eyes shut, as they have been so often lately. But it will be the glasses missing from his forehead, the book from his lap, and the right hand poised as if holding a cigarette, but without the cigarette, that will, at a glance, make me feel like I'm looking at a simulacrum, at a touched-up funerary statue of my father. Apart from that he'll be in his usual beige pyjamas, and his face will have the greyish colour of the dead that, day after day, he was already beginning to acquire in life. I will stand there a while in a daze, one pace away from that deceased father of mine, whose cheeks and hair Mother will still be stroking. When she goes downstairs to fetch water and coffee, I will want to kiss him as I have never allowed myself to do, but the contact with his cold forehead will repulse me. And as I back away I'll bump into the fat man, an undertaker who will have just received the death certificate from the doctor so he can get the paperwork moving at the notary's office early the next morning. And who will take the opportunity to show me the different coffins in his catalogue: *Colonial: Cr$ 1300.00, Prestige: Cr$ 1500.00, Chancellor: Cr$ 1750.00* . . . If it weren't for Mother I'd go outside for a breath of fresh air, or have a drink at the Riviera, or find a cinema with a midnight showing, or strike up a conversation with a passer-by: Do you know where Avenida Paulista is? Are you headed that way?

Thanks, you see my dad died. Then perhaps I'd let it all out in a sob, as I barely manage to contain my tears now on Christian's bed while translating my father's letters for him. And when I stumble over the incomplete sentences, I understand that here Father stopped writing so as not to cry himself, out of anger, out of humiliation. When I finish reading Christian is staring at the floor, shaking his head, and I am prepared to hear a harsh appraisal of the situation. Glad tidings aren't Christian's strong point, and, indeed, he believes that the chances of the boy having escaped misfortune are remote, especially if he looked anything like me. He goes on to argue that, were the boy alive, he'd have discovered his father's identity by now and, with the help of the Brazilian embassy, could have located the renowned scholar Sergio de Hollander without any difficulty. One can only conclude that Sergio Ernst isn't interested in this reunion, whether because he is now a bitter man, resentful of his father, or because he has become a prosperous man, disdainful of Third World relatives. Whatever the reason, Christian bets I won't have the time or the head for these stories of a German brother, now that Father's library will be mine. I'll be too busy contemplating it, and will even be so presumptuous as to think I can read and absorb all of his books, which Mother will bring me before I even ask for them. Speaking of which, I should do all I can to take good care of Mother, because in the case of couples as deeply intertwined as my parents, according to Christian, widowhood tends to be brief. He offers to reorganize my books for me when Mother eventually passes away, a bizarre pastime for one who grew up in a house devoid of bookshelves. After work at the Alliance Française, he will always be available to keep me company in the study or at a bistro of my choice. And, as soon as he moves into a bachelor's pad, I'll be able to visit him at all hours without any awkwardness, pretexts, ruses; no more girlfriends-for-hire or phony publishers. I look at my watch, make as if I am about to leave, but Christian holds my arm and tells me that he's been thinking about quitting the Alliance as there is a high demand for private lessons. He could even send some students my way and, if I agreed, he could get us a licence to run a language course out of my house. We'd still have evenings and nights to get serious about our literary projects. He is counting on me to cast a critical eye over his poetry, because I already proved that I am a sensitive soul when I gave him Rimbaud's little book. In exchange, he would encourage me to apply myself, for example, to a coming-of-age novel in which I deal with my troubled childhood, my family conflicts, my romantic impasses. Christian's lisping monologue in my ear begins to bother me: a jumble of words in which he alternates between Portuguese and French at random. And when, with his hand on my knee, he says that I mustn't leave out my teenage anxieties, my conflicted sexuality, my attraction to other boys, I stand up somewhat abruptly. I worry for a moment that I may have offended him over nothing, but he reacts naturally: Off already? He starts leafing through his Pushkin and without looking up tells me to leave quietly so I don't wake his parents. It isn't necessary, because halfway down the stairs I see lights on and hear meows and an old man grumbling. And it's almost

endearing to see Heinz Borgart squatting in his underwear in the kitchen, pouring a little milk from his glass
into the cat's dish. In any other situation perhaps I
wouldn't have had the audacity to speak to him: Maestro
Beauregard? The cat's fur stands on end, as Beauregard
straightens up and interrogates me with a harsh accent:
What are you doing here? Did you come in the window?
I apologize to him and admit that I've been impertinent.
In my eagerness to speak to you I even appealed to your
wife, but Madame Beauregard made it clear that you
were not to be disturbed. Nevertheless, as a last resort
I came to see your son tonight as I thought he might be
able to tell me if Mozart's 'Türkischer Marsch' performed
by Heinz Borgart is available on record. But I was wast-
ing my time with Christian; he's never even heard of
Schubert's 'Tripelkonzert', which you recorded for the
Haydn Society. After drinking his milk the pianist looks
calmer, visibly impressed with my pronunciation of the
German names. I tell him I've followed his career for
years, ever since I read allusions to his talent in an old
letter sent to my father by Anne Ernst. You must remember Anne Ernst, sir; she's this Fräulein here with the
baby in her arms in 1931. I hand the photograph to
Heinz Borgart, who almost crushes the cat when he sits
on the stool: Ugly child . . . sturdy woman . . . 1931 . . .
but, oh! Yes, the unwed mother and her cry-baby. If I'm
not mistaken I took this picture myself. Well, I say, the
baby is my half-brother on my father's side. So your
father's that famous singer, then? According to Heinz
Borgart, it was Mrs Schmidt, or was her name Schnei-
der? Anyhow, it was the building janitor who told him

that his neighbour had got pregnant to and been abandoned by a tango singer. Or was it the film-score composer, that Jew who fled to Hollywood? Perhaps memory is also lost in translation, because once I ask him to be so kind as to speak to me in his native tongue, his story flows freely: I told the janitor, Frau Schumacher, that although I felt for my neighbour, night hours should apply to all residents. I was proud of my new apartment on Fasanenstrasse, on the top floor with a living room big enough for my Bechstein grand; I don't know if you follow. I was just peeved that I had to close the piano at 10 p.m., when no one bothered to shut the child up with a bottle, a dummy, a wad of cotton wool, something. But the baby slept all day and was up all night because music was the only thing that soothed him; at least, that was what Miss Ernst told me in the inner courtyard of the building, right here where I took this picture one summer afternoon. Mother and son lived in a ground-floor room in the second block, and my rehearsals reverberated in the courtyard as if it were an amphitheatre. From 10 p.m. onwards, when everything went quiet, she'd try to get him to sleep by singing Brahms' 'Lullaby', but the baby was discerning: one wrong note was all it took to set him off. I took pity on her and every so often would have them over to my apartment, where, with the piano muted, I would finger the last few keys, imitating a music box, until he fell asleep. And I'd start playing again every time he woke up, because without realizing it, Fräulein would raise her voice every time she started telling me about the baby's father. I can still hear her laughter as she remembered how she had fallen for him in the cafeteria of UFA, the German film company, but didn't your father ever tell you this story? When she heard the waitress say the gentleman's name, Miss Ernst understood that he was Friedrich Holländer, who had composed the music for the film *The Blue Angel*, which was being shot at the studio at that time. He, in turn, was flirting with her from a distance, mistaking her for the Austrian dancer Lily Ernst, who was perhaps acting alongside Marlene Dietrich in the cabaret scene of the same film. And after so much gazing at each other, they were already, in her words, irremediably in love by the time they were introduced: she, a typist on call for UFA's screenwriters; he, a poorly paid foreign correspondent for a South American newspaper who, for a few extra Deutsche Marks, wrote subtitles for German films in his own language. Fräulein bragged that after less than a year in Berlin her boyfriend had a perfect command of our vocabulary, being the voracious reader that he was. As a result of such intense reading, even his colloquial German was literary. Before articulating his beautiful sentences, he would transcribe and copy them out neatly in his mind, just as he would visualize on a mental screen the words she spoke to him in turn. And when she told him she was expecting his child, he spent a long time staring at her with his short-sighted eyes. It wasn't until the next day that he told her he was thrilled with the news, brought her a bouquet of violets and took her for a drink at a Biergarten. Whenever he dropped her home late at night, he was reprimanded by Frau Schumacher for singing his country's little ditties in a loud voice. And the only reason he didn't invite Fräulein home to sleep with him any more was because his room in the boarding house was filling up with books at the same rate at which her belly was swelling. But in order to be of greater assistance, when autumn came he began to spend every night with Anne, which also allowed him to save on heating. His long johns were all he had left from the previous winter, as he'd sold his woollen jumpers to settle a debt at a bookshop. And, in late October, while he was tossing up between a second-hand overcoat and a first-edition *Zarathustra*, the newspaper that had sent him to Germany recalled him to his country, which was being rocked by yet another revolution. As the first snow fell, Fräulein accompanied him on a truck to the port of Hamburg to help him dispatch a pile of trunks. And she knew she would never see him again when he climbed the stairs pulling two large suitcases behind him and, forgetting to wave, disappeared onto the gangway of the ship where she, eight or so months pregnant, obviously couldn't embark. All in all, Borgart concluded, if it's news of the people in this photograph you're after, I haven't much more to offer you. After telling me her love story, Miss Ernst became taciturn during her visits and would often fall asleep on my sofa curled up with her son. And when I told her I was going away to teach at the Cologne conservatoire, she said with a vibrato in her voice: It's always the way, it's always the way. I thought her eyes were watering because of the baby who wouldn't sleep, whom I left a music box as a gift. I was sure the little one had a strong vocation for music and even promised to give him piano lessons when I returned to Berlin. And in my second year I resigned from the conservatoire, for, much as I love Wagner, I wasn't allowed to introduce my students to composers such as Mendelssohn or Mahler, who were banned by the new regime. But I had already decided to move to Paris to be with Michelle, whom I'd met at an amateur theatre festival in Cologne and who was preparing to audition for the Comédie-Française. I went to say goodbye to my mother in Berlin and, while I was there, stopped by the building on Fasanenstrasse to collect my mail and spoil Miss Ernst with an eau de cologne. But Frau Schumacher didn't work there any more and the new janitor didn't know Fräulein and her son. And you must excuse me now because I'm tired and should get back to bed. Take your photograph, have a good night, and the next time you want to get together with my son, please do it in a hotel or any old dive, just as long as it's far from here, if you follow me. Oh, and the 'Tripelkonzert' you referred to must be Schubert's 'Drei Klavierstücke'. And, yes, my congratulations to your father, because Anne was a very interesting woman. Watch your step, the lamppost is not working. *Psst.* Inside, Piaf.

Life is but a long loss of those whom we love, said Victor Hugo. And with the words of the immortal Frenchman, I mourn, in the name of the Brazilian Academy of Letters, the illustrious scholar who now leaves us, Sergio de Hollander. An assistant of the speaker leads a round of applause that doesn't gain traction because those present can't let go of the umbrellas that are barely shielding them from the storm. I calculate at least a hundred heads under a sea of black umbrellas, like a long, vaulted Gothic ceiling, not far beneath the ceiling of leaden clouds. Amidst that crowd of shadows it seems to me that I can see Stefan Zweig, Hemingway, F. Scott Fitzgerald without Zelda; I even glimpse an Oscar Wilde in a velvet jacket further back. But in reality not even Father's writer friends are in attendance. The few who are still alive live in Rio and planes don't take off in weather like this. I presume that these are old admirers of his writing, in addition to retired librarians, former bookbinders, ex-museum archivists and conservators, people in dark clothing who, after the eulogy, take turns at the graveside to pay their respects to Mother. I get one or two nods. Leaning on Vicar Bonnet, Mother doesn't really seem to notice them. She has been somewhat groggy since the wake, when I made her take one of Father's diazepams. A large crowd is still around us when people step aside for an individual with his hands free, his bodyguards' umbrellas competing with one another. It is a chief of staff bringing the state governor's condolences to Sergio de Hollander's widow. And behind this senior official appears a soaking-wet Eleonora Fortunato in an already-transparent white T-shirt with her son's face superimposed over a pair of braless, still-perky breasts: Your Excellency, please send my regards to your wife, Analu. I will indeed, thank you, thank you. If Analu doesn't remember Eleonora Fortunato, we were introduced at the Petite Galerie by Ulrich Reichel, her German lover. After a heavy silence a woman speaks: But how rude! Rude? I'll tell you what's rude. It's this government not even releasing Assunta's son for his father's funeral. The chief of staff beats a retreat with his entourage, then the other umbrellas turn one after another like gears and disperse down the cemetery paths.

16

Mr Hollander is a dickhead! No matter how deplorable my readers were, I published their considerations *ipsis litteris* and never shrank from a democratic exchange: *I suggest you read some Machado de Assis, my esteemed and illiterate Mr J.B. I suggest you stick Machado de Assis up you're [sic] arse, Mr Hollander!!!* In the beginning I wrote a few pieces to nobody but myself, modelling them on my brother's jottings in his school notebooks. Then I began to receive essays from readers in even more atrocious Portuguese, which almost led me to abandon my selfless work. I corrected them with some degree of impatience, often eliciting ill-mannered replies, followed by caustic remarks from third parties, but ultimately it was always the same members of a small community. Until a veteran journalist from *A Gazeta* published a note in a popular weekly saying that the name of my sorely missed father was being tarnished in the blog of an opportunistic and pedantic grammarian. From then on, as predicted by Natércia, my followers multiplied, there was an upswing in the number of insults being exchanged, I attracted more and more advertisers, and actually built up a bit of a nest egg. I had gone to Professor Natércia after Mother's death, when Father's pension expired and I found myself in a tight spot. Having books as my sole occupation was becoming unsustainable. Theoretically, relieving myself of my inheritance would allow me to enjoy it. At worst it would be like trying to save a floating library by bailing into the sea the very books that gave my voyage its meaning. To stall for time, I toyed with the idea of selling to a second-hand bookshop a few kilos of novels that I knew back to front, but leafing through them I realized I only remembered fragments of their narratives, characters' names, characters from other books, random phrases, flashes, the cinders of a dream. And hovering over my shoulders there was still the shadow of Mother, who would have been horrified to see the library carved up, not least because she admired it more from the outside than from the inside. Determined to preserve it in its entirety, she had even chased off one of Father's rival bibliophiles, who, on the very morning of his wake, had settled his hungry gaze upon the eleven sixteenth-century volumes in the bookcase in the sitting room. The snoop started sending her chocolates, dropping in at the most inappropriate hours, and didn't even wait for her mourning to ease before making her a proposal in US dollars for the whole lot. I understand that Mother was offended, but after so many years with Father, she should have known that a man with a lust for books is always prone to losing his composure. And I have to admit that sometimes Mother was a little too naive, because leaving precious works like those, their leather covers gleaming with beeswax, in the full view of a collector, was like polishing up cherubs for a pervert. But I think that, for her, caring for the books was a matter of taking pride in appearances, as innocent as doing her hair, for deep down she always knew that Father, although a doting husband, couldn't distinguish very well between her and the library. And she wasn't about to let it go to seed just because he was no longer there in the flesh; on the contrary, she had even more time to devote to tidying the house after she gave up the fruit pies and traded home-made pasta for the mass-produced variety. Although she could barely see a thing any more, she would climb the five-rung stepladder with cloth and brush to dust off the most recondite volumes, wipe down their covers and spines, sniff them for fungi and silverfish and then return them to their posts. I followed her around with outstretched arms as a precaution, and one day when she was going through the bookcase in the hallway, I noticed she was preoccuped with some Brits at the back of the shelf, among which was *The Golden Bough.* Mother didn't usually disturb the insides of the books, where even the most banal traces of Father were sacred. But this time she opened, sniffed, sniffed again and shook *The Golden Bough* until Anne Ernst's letter came loose and fell to the ground. And her ears, which were growing sharper by the day, in contrast to her diminishing sight, detected the sound of the envelope landing: What was that noise? It's a letter in German to Father. Want me to read it? *Berlin, 21 December 1931. Dear Sergio, From your Silence I gather you are as always in your Books immersed. Desolate . . .* When I saw that Mother was barely able to keep her balance at the top of the stepladder, looking at me with her clouded eyes, I went on: *Desolate that I can no longer get lost with you in the streets of Kreuzberg, wishing you a happy 1932. With friendship and admiration, Walter Benjamin.* In the past I wouldn't have missed the opportunity to read Anne's letter to my mother from start to finish so as to bring up Sergio Ernst in conversation once and for all. I could even have shown her the photograph of Father in Berlin with Anne in the family way, in exchange for some relevant secrets that she might be able to disclose. But by now it was hardly appropriate to go questioning Mother about a long-lost brother in Germany, when she was suffering more and more for lack of news of her own son. It was a rare night that she didn't go down to open the door for him, awoken by a car horn or a possum scuttling outside. She often came into his old room in the dead of the night, too, creeping over slowly to touch my unkempt hair and convince herself that it wasn't him sleeping there. I couldn't even greet her when I came home, because when she heard my cheerful voice downstairs she would lean over the banister: Mimmo? Then she'd accuse me of playing tricks on her, as if it weren't enough that I'd already led her on with fanciful tales from Argentina: Deceiving a blind woman is a sin, Ciccio! And Dr Zuzarte's insistence that her cataracts could be cured with a simple operation was in vain. Why should I want my sight back, she would ask, to give myself a fright in the mirror? She used a white cane to go to church, felt her way around the house with a broom and, unerring with the salt, cooked while listening attentively to the news on the radio. She who had never paid attention to politics now knew congressmen, ministers and high-ranking army, navy and air force brass by name. She thought President Médici was more sinister than Mussolini, but turned up the volume whenever the advert from the government came on, because Mimmo's voice-over was still being used: He who does not live to serve Brazil does not deserve to live in Brazil. In the morning she would ask me to read her the newspapers and open letters, which consisted mostly of books that publishers continued to send to Father. And then, one day, among junk mail and electricity and gas bills, I found in my hands a blue-and-white-edged envelope addressed to Assunta de Hollander: *Caspita*, Mamma, here's a letter from Argentina! To which she replied: *Macché* Argentina, Ciccio, don't pull my leg. But it was indeed a letter from Eleonora Fortunato in Argentina, inviting her to a private viewing at the Galería Bonino in Buenos Aires, where she was exhibiting her latest collages explicitly inspired by her son's suffering. A valiant woman like Anita Garibaldi, Mother said. If I weren't so decrepit, I'd get out there with Eleonora in defence of my son, I'd let *tutto il mondo* know, just like her. Through hints like that, Mother was trying to chastise me for spending my days in the lounge chair, instead of engaging in goodness knows what action. One night at dinner, she let slip that she'd be satisfied if I devoted myself half as much to Mimmo as I did to the other one. What other one? I asked with a start. What other one, Mamma? She said nothing and started plucking at breadcrumbs on the tablecloth. But, like Eleonora Fortunato, I really believed that after giving a statement, having the fright put in him once or twice and serving a little time, my brother would be released without having come to any great harm, given how obviously ignorant he was of political matters. He would also be able to count on the testimony of Beatriz Alessandri, who would be ready to exculpate the gentleman who had offered to carry her backpack. Tricita would repudiate any suggestion of intimate relations with Domingos de Hollander, and wouldn't need too much coercion, undressing and violation to give up the name of her fiancé, who had already fallen from grace and wouldn't receive any supplementary punishment for being engaged to a mere Argentinian carrier pigeon. As a routine procedure, in one last interview they would ask my brother if he happened to be acquainted with a certain Ariosto Fortunato, which he would naturally deny. Unless, out of excessive zeal, or imagining his testicles being strangled in a tourniquet, he confessed that he did know said individual by sight. Ariosto Fortunato was friends with his brother, Francisco de Hollander, otherwise known as Ciccio. Then he would be released, perhaps even catch a lift with one Inspector Borges and when he knocked at the door he would announce himself in a loud voice: Morning, Mamma! You're going to drive me crazy, Ciccio, Mother would say, but when he lifted her up and twirled her around the sitting room, she would exclaim: Mimmo! She would run her fingers through his hair and shriek: Madonna, it's Mimmo himself! And she would call me to embrace him: *Subito, Ciccio, è il tuo fratello!* But I'd no longer be there; Inspector Borges would have hauled me off for a chat at the army headquarters. Tied to a metal seat, a bunch of wires attached to my naked body, it's natural that I'd have a lot to say about my best friend, a man with balls, in the words of his torturers, who took, without spilling his guts, what no one can take, and who ended his days like a zombie from so many blows to the head and so much pentothal in his veins. I, on the other hand, subjected to intermittent electrical charges, unsure whether the pain itself or the expectation of it was more unbearable, had no intention of becoming a hero of the resistance. But there would be no way for me to cooperate with the interrogation if I knew nothing of my friend's transgressions, his comrades in arms, their meeting places, his group's organigram, their contacts abroad, their *noms de guerre*. The only thing that would come to mind would be secrets from my childhood spent with Bugs Bunny, Captain Marvel, Plastic Man *et al.*, and when he heard my stammering the furious major would wind the handcrank faster to intensify the electric current, which would bring on vomiting, convulsions and, suddenly, a heart attack. Now look what you've done, you fuckwit, the colonel would say, and the fuckwit major would try to resuscitate me with a new round of shocks, before sending for the doctor, by which time there would be nothing to be done. When he saw me there with a crooked head and glassy eyes, Dr Zuzarte would say, But didn't I warn you the lad had a weak heart? What now? And now they would dump my body in a police van with fake plates, which would carry me along four hundred kilometres of motorway to a beach at dawn. And only like this would I arrive at the Copacabana that Maria Helena had told me so much about, with the salty air that she described as the breath of the waves, although fouled by the odours of my body and others laid out on the sand. The vultures would be beaten off with an oar by a ferryman, who, after wrenching from our mouths the gold teeth that would repay him for his labour, would carry us over his shoulder, pile us up on his barge and, on the high seas, serve us to his brothers the fish. And when she awoke from a bad dream like this, Mother would take it as a divine warning, and fly into a panic, and cry to the heavens, and between sobs communicate to my brother that his brother was dead. A little calmer now, after a visit from Vicar Bonnet, she would bid Mimmo farewell and beg him to understand, because without Ciccio she had lost her will to live. And my brother would be left to roam alone that outlandish house, to him as big as it was suffocating, surrounded by books as impenetrable as wallpaper. He would avoid the kitchen and the study, and he'd more or less come to terms with the loss of his parents, but he'd be surprised to find himself deeply missing someone about whom he'd thought he'd never given a *cazzo*. He would burst into my room, rummage through my drawers, search in vain for a picture of me, any old passport pic. Having forgotten my face, he would look at himself in the mirror, face on, in profile, he'd part his hair on one side, then the other, and he wouldn't find himself as good-looking as before, when he had me around for comparison. Over the phone he would entice into his lair one, two, three hundred women who perhaps wouldn't give him the same pleasure as before, now that I no longer came to masturbate outside his door. He would want to eliminate me from his thoughts, liquidate the house and move into a serviced apartment, but the real-estate agent would tell him that without my signature it would be impossible to sell. He would eventually discover that the library was not part of the estate, and would have no qualms about flogging it, perhaps to the Calouste Gulbenkian Foundation, flabbergasted to find that the collection was worth more than the house itself. And, once hollow, perhaps the house would collapse. Without that mass of literature, its skeleton of bookcases might bend and snap, but these absurdities can only be the product of my sick dreams, if not a posthumous nightmare of Mother's. What really happened was that after Mother died from missing Mimmo, I was strapped for cash and remembered Professor Natércia, who had close ties with the chancellor's office at the University of São Paulo. I phoned her to ask if the university might be interested in renting the residence of Sergio de Hollander to establish a cultural centre where I'd be allowed to live and read my books without being disturbed. She came to see the house of her salacious memories once again, and, pushing fifty, Natércia was in good shape. She went to bed with me once, twice, got hooked, visited me every afternoon; meanwhile negotiations with the university became bogged down in bureaucracy. And I was already considering going back to teaching a preparatory course, when she showed up with an outdated computer that had belonged to her husband, who was by now quite long in the tooth. She got rid of Father's Remington, had an Internet connection installed in the study, created the webpage *Hollander's Guide to Better Writing* and was a gifted lover until she was widowed, married another old man and disappeared from my life. Natércia was an educated woman, a polyglot, and Mother would have enjoyed talking to her. She'd have found her Italian cute, with that farm-girl drawl Natércia had never lost. I honestly believe that in life Mother never got used to the absence of women's voices coming from Mimmo's room, because every so often she'd ask me about this one or that one who'd frequented it. I'd go looking for his exes in the bars of old, but I couldn't even find the bars because they're always changing locations in the São Paulo night, except for the occasional establishment which allows itself to sink into decline, taking its captive audience of half a dozen regulars with it. In my wanderings I even ended up on the Beauregards' drab street, where their house had given way to a Shell petrol station. The alleyway had been widened and was now an avenue with nightclubs and music halls packed with dancing girls who looked right through me and had no idea who my brother was. I only found women of my league in the most obscure corners of the city centre, and I asked them to be discreet because Mother would have frowned at the language they used. Mother pretended to ignore my bringing whores into the house and merely commented now and then that a woman who wore very sweet perfume was not good marriage material. She also played dumb when, as I read out her bank statements to her, I omitted my withdrawals for personal expenses, or when I spared her the most depressing articles from the newspaper. But I couldn't prevent her from listening to the radio and hearing about the death of Eleonora Fortunato, who was hit by a car in front of Cemitério da Consolação. She also heard an interview with a witness to the accident, a night guard according to whom the bedraggled artist had been staggering along after midnight, before throwing herself under the wheels of a Kombi that didn't stop to offer help. It's a pity, said the reporter, but from what I know the prize-winning painter had a problem with alcohol and had suffered from psychological disorders ever since her son was arrested for car theft. Incensed, Mother turned off the radio, never listened to the news again and around the same time began to receive messages from the other side. It was Fortunato, it was Father, it was her mother, Donatella, it was even her wretched father, Pandolfo; they all came to gesticulate at her bedside wearing looks of consternation, as if trying to find the words to relay the unspeakable. *Basta! Via! Fuori! Fuori!* She would send them away and her cries would go right through me as I lay in my room.

I agreed to sleep in her bed with her, where, fearful, she struggled to stay awake and wouldn't let me sleep. She would press her ear to my chest, sniff my armpits, pat my face, hold my eyelids open and talk to me about Mimmo. Because Mimmo had the fatal air of those who died young, because Mimmo had been born with a murmur in his heart, because Mimmo had the smouldering gaze of Rudolph Valentino, who had died when he was Mimmo's age. You should have heard what a calamity the funerals held for Mimmo were, according to Mother: women threw themselves out of windows all over the world, and I was relieved when her speech grew slurred, her ideas became jumbled and finally she fell asleep. She still talked about Mimmo while dreaming and often ground her teeth, but after a time I grew accustomed to it all, except being shaken awake in the middle of the night for breakfast. We no longer kept normal hours: dinner was served before midday, we napped here and there and went to bed when it was still light out. What day is it today? she would ask. 25 January 1973.

Still? It was already late August, but I held back the calendar to ease her anxiety: What about now, what day is it? It puzzled her that time seemed to be dragging its feet lately, which was true: at our house 1973 took several years to pass. Even when the situation in the country began to ease up, it was a good thing I kept her in the dark because my brother's name wasn't on any of the lists naming those who'd been granted amnesty. And news of those returning from exile and the release of prisoners of conscience, cheerfully received by friends and relatives, might have felt, to Mother, like she was being taunted. Democracy was soon restored in Brazil and in neighbouring countries, and even the Berlin Wall came down, but I asked Mother to be patient. Mimmo still has a few more weeks of his sentence to serve, I'd tell her, although judging from photographs of the packed prisons it looked more like the hard-line military government had opted to lock up blacks rather than subversives. I tried to distract her with the same old headlines, the election of the Polish pope, Italy winning the World Cup, but in the end she no longer listened; even chopping tomatoes in the kitchen she looked like she was asleep with her eyes open, a pair of white eyes that rolled around aimlessly. In bed she began to summon up her dead, whom she hadn't seen for a while because, as often happens with those who go blind in later life, she was also losing her sight in her dreams. And she preferred her former visitors to the tormented voices she now heard, not knowing how to exorcize them in the pitch darkness. She would say the Creed in Latin, mutter insults in dialect, and one night woke me up in a state, for the voice from the other world that she'd just heard was Mimmo's. It wasn't Father, as she had first thought, if only it had been another of my pranks, but the one calling her this time was definitely Mimmo. I tried to reason with her: It was an incubus, Mother, it was just a bad dream. But there was no talking her out of it, she needed to be reunited with Mimmo, who, after a difficult time in purgatory, was waiting, like a child at the door to the cinema, for Mamma to sanction his entrance to the heavenly mansion. Vicar Bonnet, who was always caring towards Mother, came to celebrate Mass at the foot of her bed. And before receiving the holy wafer, Mother asked if it was a sin to yearn and pray for one's own death. Why no, said the priest, if even the Virgin begged her crucified son not to leave her for long in this vale of tears. When Vicar Bonnet left, Mother made me sit beside her, crossed my forehead and told me it was time I got my act together, for it was up to me to carry on the Hollander name. She placed the back of her hand on my neck and thought I was feverish, but it was only that her hand was cold. Then she crossed her hands on her chest, fixed a half-smile on her lips and her eyes finally went still. When Dr Zuzarte arrived there was little to be done. He took her pulse without conviction and struggled to close her eyelids.

I've never believed in supernatural phenomena, much less could I have imagined that a university professor like Natércia would be afraid of spooks. But we were busy on the bed once, which was rocking and creaking rhythmically, when, all of a sudden, after a kind of groan at the top of the bookcase, a hardback edition of *Don Quixote* fell to the floor. Natércia bucked me off, showed me the goose pimples on her arm and said: That was your brother. I told her it was more likely that the structure of the house had given a little, considering the condition of the wooden beams, which were infested with termites, not to mention the cracks in the walls which the books concealed. But engineering catastrophes didn't faze Natércia, who pulled me into my old room, where we went back to fooling around. She had come out with something odd once before when I had failed in bed and, for lack of anything else to say, I asked if my brother's dick was much bigger than mine. Suspecting I might be under some kind of spell, Natércia said she knew a shaman who could untie my feet and open all paths for me. At the time I thought she was joking, or just showing off her knowledge of folk-lore, but after the incident that she classified as the work of an authentic poltergeist, I abandoned my brother's room for good on her advice, without touching the *Quixote* lying at the foot of the bookcase. I only went back there to get a few changes of clothes and to see if I could find a cheque, the sort Natércia sometimes slipped under the pillow. I took those tips unwillingly, not least because the cheques were from her joint account with her husband, and the idea that the old boy was supporting me affected my performance. But Natércia was certain I would pay off my debt with interest, just as soon as I won the National Lottery. Every week she would ask if I'd remembered to check the winning numbers, even though I repeatedly told her that, unlike my brother, I didn't even know how to play the lottery. And one day, seeing me pull on a pair of trousers with poorly stitched hems, she real-

ized I'd appropriated Domingos's clothes and ordered me
to throw them out if I didn't want to die in poverty. She
took one of my old socks to the shaman so he could redo
his work, given that the items she had previously spirited
away for him to bless belonged to my brother. I had a
good laugh about that, because if the powers of her sage
were to be trusted, while I had fallen on hard times in the
terrestrial world, my brother was hitting the jackpot in
some lottery in the afterlife. But the undeniable truth is
that shortly thereafter I was catapulted from Portuguese
teacher with an obscure blog to polemical social media-
based grammar guru, sponsored, as it happens, by the
National Lottery. It wasn't just to make a living, however,
that I had begun spending hours in front of the computer,
forsaking good literature. When I was done with my
work for the day, I felt compelled to visit porn sites,
search for explicit sex videos and stay up all night
exchanging lewd messages with semi-literate partners.
And by the time I got back to the lounge chair, my eyes
were tired and my head faraway; I couldn't concentrate on
any book. I read as perhaps my brother once had, as if my
eyes slid down a sheet of transparent glass to the foot of
the page, only to return to the top of the same paragraph
without having taken anything in. I repeat that I have
never believed in witches, but, as Sancho Panza and
everyone knows, there's no denying they're real: *que las
hay, las hay.* I started putting in hourly calls to Natércia,
who, newly wed to the former chancellor and emeritus
professor of the university, told the secretary never to put
me through. May I ask who's calling? the secretary would
ask. What's it regarding? And there was no way I could

get her to give me the mobile number of Dr Natércia's witch doctor. Via the Internet, however, I contacted psychics of various persuasions who, without exception, believed I was possessed by the spirit of my brother, disembodied at the age of thirty in a sudden and violent manner. For a good while I wasted my capital on energy cures, which quite possibly neutralized one another, because each voodoo priest made it his business to mess with his predecessor's mumbo-jumbo. More recently a tarot reader texted me to say that those fools had allowed themselves to be bamboozled by an evil spirit: according to the cards my brother had passed away at fifty, after a long illness, in a foreign land. I was already thinking about looking into the matter when a clairvoyant got my home number God knows how, and no sooner had I picked up than he began to reel off the services he provided to the police: solving kidnappings, finding where people were held captive and locating criminals' hideouts. And without me asking anything, he said that a man by the name of Domingos de Hollander was roaming the outskirts of Greater São Paulo with no memory. For more detailed information he would need an image of him, like a composite sketch that I could get done by a civil police artist. Without thinking twice, I promised to email the clairvoyant a photograph of my missing brother, like the one in Mother's picture frame, posing à la Rock Hudson. But when I scanned it I realized that no one would recognize my brother, to me forever young like a character in a novel, from that Don Juan of the 1970s. So I aged his portrait with the help of a high-tech program that I worked out how to download onto my computer. In a matter of seconds I saw his voluptuous lips wither, I saw his eyes sink into his head and lose their sparkle, I saw his ears grow long and his cheeks flaccid, I saw oily bumps on his bulbous nose, all over his skin I saw the blotches and fissures with which time punishes human beauty. I made his thick hair grey, then completely white; still not satisfied I gave him a receding hairline, yanked out tufts, made him bald, yellowed him a little and sent him to the clairvoyant. The clairvoyant didn't reply, so from time to time I sent new messages, produced upcycled versions of my brother, by now in his seventies, until I realized that it was very much in the interest of these police collaborators, leftovers from the dictatorship, to delude me with futile hopes. The theory that my brother had been shuffling here and there for forty years seemed to me as ludicrous as explanations of a cosmic nature. I had written it all off and had returned to my work and solitary pleasures, when just the other day someone rang the doorbell outside normal pizza delivery hours. I saw before me a bald man, tall like my brother but slightly hunchbacked, his face even more worn than the portraits I had forged on my computer, his left cheek sporting the vestige of a scar disguised by a web of wrinkles. He apologized, it was a mistake, he was looking for an old resident of that house by the name of Francisco, and I suddenly discovered that I was face to face with Udo Reichel, who had lost his hair but not the habit of puffing at it. I invited him in, forgetting I had no whisky, or beer, or even coffee to offer him, nor could I ask him to take a seat on the furniture piled high with books that I never unwrapped. We ended up sitting on two boxes in the sitting room, smoking and staring at the floor, until he broke the silence by stomping on a large cockroach. Then he asked if I lived alone, aside from the cockroaches, laughed at the joke and asked after my brother; Udo's the sort who asks a lot of questions but doesn't care about the answers. I told him that Domingos had left the house with Ariosto's girlfriend one day, never to be seen again, but he was referring to my German brother, the one with the avocado-shaped head. I knew nothing of Sergio Ernst either; I feared the worst, and when I started telling him about the Jewish children on the death trains, he interrupted me to talk about his alleged brothers who were also a pain in the arse. He said that every other day some bastard would bring a new court action to get him to take a DNA test. Suit by suit, settlement by settlement, and including his money-grabbing lawyers' fees, they had already whittled away much of his inheritance from his father, who had died last year at the age of 101, still active, with a penile prosthesis that he'd had implanted at ninety-five. And, apart from women's arses, old Reichel's other fetish was World War II relics. He collected military medals, cartridge belts, paratroopers' buckles, Gestapo insignias, miniature panzers, fighter jets and bombers, in addition to piles and piles of German newspapers, photographs and period documents, among which was a letter that might be of some value to me. The minute Udo pulled the folded sheet of airmail paper out of his pocket, I recognized in reverse the Berlin City letterhead from the document that the police had taken so many years ago from Mimmo's drawer.

Stadt Berlin / Bezirksamt Tiergarten

Jugendamt, Amtsvormundschaft

Postanschrift des Absenders: Fernruf: C 9 Tiergarten 0013, Apparat......**94**
Bezirksamt Tiergarten, Berlin NW 21, Alt-Moabit 94

Herrn
    Sergio de Hollander

    <u>Rio de Janeiro</u>
    39, Rio Maria Angelica
    <u>Südamerika</u>

Ihr Zeichen: Ihre Nachricht vom: Unser Zeichen: Tag: 24.9.1934

B. A. Tierg. Jug. 2 E 146

Betrifft:

        Sehr geehrter Herr de Hollander!

        Bereits vor Jahren habe ich versucht, durch Vermittlung der
deutschen Gesandtschaft in Rio de Janeiro mit Ihnen in Verbindung
zu treten, um für meinen Mündel Sergio Ernst, dessen Erzeuger Sie
sind, Unterhaltsgelder von Ihnen zu erlangen. Leider war dieser
Versuch vergeblich. Wenn ich mich nun heute nochmals mit Ihnen in
Verbindung setze, so geschieht es in der Annahme, dass es auch Ihr
Wunsch ist, dass dem von Ihnen erzeugten Kinde eine gute und dau-
ernde Heimat und eine geordnete Erziehung wird.

        Sergio Ernst, geb. 21.12.1930, befindet sich bei den Eheleuten
Günther, NO 50, Greifswalder Str. 212/13, 2.Hof, seit geraumer
Zeit in Pflege. Das Ehepaar gewann den Jungen lieb und trägt sich
mit dem Gedanken, ihn an Kindesstatt anzunehmen. Der Adoptionsver-
trag wurde geschlossen, auch vormundschaftsgerichtlich genehmigt
und liegt augenblicklich beim Amtsgericht Berlin zur Dispensertei-
lung des vollendeten 50.Lebensjahres und zur Bestätigung.

        Das Bestätigungsgericht verlangt nun den Nachweis der arischen

                                      <u>Abstammung</u>

Anlagen

                                   Bei Antwort und Geldsendungen wird um
                                   Angabe obigen Geschäftszeichens gebeten.

Abstammung. Dieser kann nach der Mutter geführt werden. Der
Junge muss aber auch nach seinem Vater Arier sein. Ich muss
Sie daher bitten, mir Ihre Geburtsurkunde, die Geburtsurkunden
Ihrer Eltern und die Geburtsurkunden Ihrer beiderseitigen
Grosseltern zuzusenden. Aus diesen Urkunden muss die Religion
Ihrer Vorfahren zu ersehen sein.

In der Annahme, dass Sie sich dieser meiner Aufforderung
im Interesse des Jungen nicht verschliessen, hoffe ich von
Ihnen zu hören und sehe dem Eingang der Urkunden entgegen.

Mit dem deutschen Gruss

Heil Hitler!

I.A.

Leitender Stadtvormund

Deputy Mayor
of the Regional Administration of Tiergarten, Berlin
City of Berlin/Tiergarten Town Hall
Secretariat for Childhood and Youth, Child Welfare

To Mr
Sergio de Hollander
Rio de Janeiro
Rua Maria Angélica, 39
South America

24.9.1934

Dear Mr de Hollander!

   Some years ago I tried to reach you through the German Legation in Rio de Janeiro to request child support for my ward Sergio Ernst, of whom you are the biological father. Unfortunately, my attempt was in vain. Thus, if I am contacting you again today, I do so in the belief that it is your wish too that the child you fathered gets a good permanent home and a proper education.

   For some time now, Sergio Ernst, born on 21 December 1930, has been living in the care of the Günthers, No. 50, Greifswalder Strasse 212/13, courtyard 2. The couple have grown fond of the boy and want to adopt him. The adoption contract has been signed, custody has been authorized by a judge, and the document is currently at the Berlin Regional Court, for the granting of a waiver of the minimum age of fifty and for legitimation.

   The court of legitimation is now requesting proof

of Aryan origin. This can be demonstrated on the mother's side. But the boy also has to be of Aryan descent on the father's side. As such, I must ask you to send me your birth certificate, your parents' birth certificates and those of your maternal and paternal grandparents. From these certificates it should be possible to infer your forefathers' religion.

Confident that, in the boy's interest, you will not refuse my request, I look forward to hearing from you and await the arrival of the certificates.

With the German greeting,
Heil Hitler!
pp
Municipal Welfare Officer

17

Late in the afternoon of 20 May 2013 I board my
Lufthansa flight knowing I won't get any sleep. I didn't
know aeroplane seats were such a tight squeeze, nor that
a German beanpole was going to invade my space with
his right knee. But after dreaming about this trip for
nights on end, I couldn't possibly close my eyes now that
I am making it, even if I were stretched out in first class.
I reserved a window seat in the hope that I might see the
ocean, but the plane has barely taken off when it pierces
the clouds. Above the clouds, at cruising altitude and
speed, we more or less follow the Brazilian coast, which
Father's ship skirted in 1929. I consult our route in the
in-flight magazine with the funny feeling that I am
retracing by air, at almost seventy, the path my father
took before the age of thirty. I can even boast that I have
probably read all of the books that would have been
scattered about his cabin, in addition to so many others
that he would only come to know later: Have you read
Kafka, Sergio? So what are you waiting for? On his way
to Europe Father would still have been occupied with
German grammars; at the most he'd have had a go at
some children's fables with a dictionary on his lap. And
he'd have worked overtime trying to understand what the

hell this letter is all about, if he could have foreseen it in my hands, with his name at the top and signed with a *Heil Hitler*. After refusing dinner, I accept a beer and rest on the fold-out tray the flimsy piece of paper typed on both sides, which is almost falling to pieces. It is full of creases, as if it has been folded and refolded in different pockets, flattened inside a book beneath books, stretched in a wallet behind banknotes, let's say Deutsche Marks. Lately I've come to suspect that Father returned to Germany with this letter immediately after the war on a propeller plane that made multiple stops. I have no way of confirming that such a journey took place; it would have been prior to my earliest memories and was never mentioned at home. But I can imagine him in a taxi, chain-smoking amid the debris and dust in the eastern sector of Berlin, on his way to the home of the couple who had a few years earlier grown so fond of his son. From what I read in an online encyclopaedia, a cigarette factory was in business at the Günthers' address until the mid-1930s, when it was repurposed to make military uniforms. I presume that Mr Günther, kept on as janitor or manager of a certain uniform service to the Reich, was charged with supervising the sewing rooms, packaging, storage and loading of goods onto armed forces vehicles. Uniforms left Greifswalder Strasse 212/13 to conquer Europe, grey-green dolmans from its workshops paraded down the Champs-Élysées of occupied Paris. The feared black garments of the SS may also have come out of there, in addition to woollen overcoats that became bloodied and mutilated, or froze with their owners, or were buried along with them on the steppes of Russia.

After Germany surrendered, batches of uniforms and fabric cuttings must have remained in stock and the Günthers wouldn't have known what to do with them. And still reeling from the last rounds of bombing, perhaps horrified by revelations of their country's recent past, they'd have reluctantly opened the door to that middle-aged man, perhaps a Soviet secret service agent, asking in a deep voice and strong accent for Mr Günther. But as soon as he identified himself as Sergio de Hollander, from Brazil, South America, he'd have been told to scram by the indignant owner of the house. And Mrs Günther wouldn't have hesitated to report the stranger to the police to prevent him from approaching a minor with sinister intentions. However, considering that the couple only had temporary custody of the child in 1934, and that years later Father still hadn't gathered all the documents requested by the court of adoption, it seems more likely that the Günthers would have returned my brother to the children's home at some point, in exchange for an orphan of proven pedigree. And they'd have barely been able to remember the little Brazilian by the time Father knocked at the door, identifying himself as Sergio de Hollander, from Brazil, South America. But they would have been courteous, offered him a seat, served him a cup of watery coffee and wouldn't have concealed their pride when they introduced him to their heir, a blond boy with chiselled features and blue eyes. Distraught, Father must have gone straight to the Secretariat for Childhood and Youth, determined to take Sergio Ernst with him if he was there, now almost fifteen years old, still waiting for a kind soul to give him a home. He didn't find him, just as perhaps he found nothing but the ruins of the Secretariat building, and then he'd have wondered if his son hadn't been recruited at the end of the war, like so many young men in short trousers, to face the tanks of the Red Army. And if he had lost his life in the last battle of Berlin, as so many others had, a relative should have been notified by now. Already braced for the painful news, Father would have knocked at the door of his old love nest at Fasanenstrasse 22 and staggered back in horror, momentarily convinced that the woman smiling at him with only two teeth in her mouth was the mother of his son. But it would only have been a friendly old lady who wouldn't have refused him the use of her phonebook: *Ernst, Ernst, Ernst, Ernst, Ernst*, and among dozens of Ernsts there would have been a Miss Anne Ernst, at such-and-such a phone number, such-and-such an address. He'd have got no dialling tone on the old woman's phone, nor on the phones at the few cafes he found open, and exploring a string of public phone booths that were out of order he'd have arrived at the address he had jotted down, where, quite possibly, a gramophone was playing the waltz from *The Blue Angel*: *Love's always been my game / Play it how I may* . . . But as for what went on inside that house, I don't dare speculate. I only imagine that Mother was beginning to fret about the time her husband was taking, since he may have told her he was just going to pop over to Paris quickly for a scholarly conference or a class at the Sorbonne. And when he returned home after a month or more, she'd merely have asked: Sergio, did you find what you were looking for? And Father would have replied: No, Assunta.

Sergio? Planted in front of the hotel with Father's posture, left arm bent behind his back, the old man takes a puff on his cigarette and doesn't turn around. On my way there from the airport, I regret not having asked the taxi to pull over at a bus stop when I saw a man in his eighties, as my German brother would be today, reading a newspaper with his glasses pushed up on his forehead. Sergio! I repeat to the old smoker, and a porter asks if he can take the decrepit wooden suitcase that Father inherited from my grandfather inside on a trolley. I enter the hotel through the revolving door and immediately feel underdressed. The Adlon, which burned down in 1945, was rebuilt inspired by the original architecture, and its beautifully decorated interiors must be like the ones Father saw the day he came here in December 1929. And the beautiful girls at the counter must also be of the same lineage as the ones that Father, then a shy foreign correspondent, addressed when he came to see Mr Thomas Mann, not even sure they would help him. Welcome to the Adlon, Mr Hollander, says the receptionist in English as she hands me back my passport along with the magnetic card to my room. I tip the porter but don't go up to my room; instead, I take a taxi to Greifswalder Strasse 212/13 before it gets dark. And even if I never learn what became of my brother, this trip has already been worth it, just to be able to wander alone through the courtyard, covered with construction material and rubble from renovations. Scaffolding and hoarding panels mask the facade of the rear building which, after the renovations, will no doubt be used for some kind of venture which I seriously doubt will work. Not so long ago the

Magnet club enjoyed fleeting success here, replacing the obscure Miles nightclub, which stood elbow-to-elbow with the tiny Eigenreich Theatre, which replaced rooms to let for artists and students, which succeeded a plus-size women's clothing factory, which went bankrupt when the country was reunified. But back when my brother came to live here, the building must still have been used for its true function, as the Problem cigarette factory. Yes, Problem. This was the prophetic brand of cigarettes produced by a Jew in this 1920s art deco building, designed by another Jew, Ernst Ludwig Freud, father of the painter and son of Dr Sigmund. And if I know Father, he'd have been thoroughly amused to smoke cigarettes called Problem, which, to make an obscure olfactory association, would have given his room in the Berlin boarding house the same smell of Turkish tobacco that would have permeated Sergio Ernst's child-hood memories. Sergio Ernst! The name echoing in the courtyard slipped out of my mouth accidentally, because the man I saw in a flurry of activity on the other side of the street is just a kid, who now crosses over as if heeding my call. Sorry to bother you, he says in faltering German, but do you know where Heinrich-Roller-Strasse is? According to my pocket guide it is just a little further along, the second street on the right, but I offer to accompany him because he doesn't seem to understand. He says he's confused by the street numbering, which doesn't have odd numbers on one side and even numbers on the other; instead, they go up on one side and down on the other. Ah, there it is! says the young man, who hurries down the side street towards a tavern called Vinería

Carvalho, where he is greeted at the door by another young man who looks Spanish, with tanned cheeks. Still suffering from jet lag and the night without sleep, I intended to return to my hotel early, but the wines and cold cuts on display are appealing. And the Spaniard suggests a Rioja with a plate of tapas, which he will serve me in the back room right away. There, a table is occupied by a group of people with the somewhat careless appearance of the retired, among whom there is a portly gentleman who croons: *The young folk are all dancing / The Lipsi with great passion / The youths just love this rhythm / The Lipsi is the fashion.* Highly focused, elbows held wide, he entertains his friends with a finger dance on the table-top, simulating the synchronized steps of a pair dancing the Lipsi: *Only to the Lipsi / Do our couples dance / The rumba and the cha-cha-cha do not stand a chance.* Can someone tell me what this is all about? I ask, and in the chair at the head of the table a chap with dyed hair explains that the Lipsi was a style of music created in East Germany in an effort to sideline Elvis Presley's rock and roll. Priceless! I say, *fantastisch!* but when I am about to ask the man to repeat his number, the subject of the conversation changes to the football of the 1960s. The table is divided between supporters of Lokomotive Leipzig and Dynamo Berlin, and I take advantage of the situation to declare myself a fanatical supporter of Santos Futebol Clube, which won the World Cup with Pelé. I'm Brazilian, I swear, I learned this fluent German of mine from my father, who lived here before the war and was pals with Thomas Mann. He even had a son in Berlin whom I've spent years looking for, but before I can get into the story, the fat guy gets up and goes to the toilet, others head outside to smoke and a big man with a goatee asks the Spaniard for the bill. In the end the only one left at the table is the man with the pitch-black hair, who, while fiddling on a laptop, tells me he visited Brazil once, swam in the sea at Copacabana and watched a show of *mulattas*. But it wasn't tourism that took him to Rio; rather, he was looking for some family names that he'd had a hard time tracking down in the mess that was the local archives. He is my age or a little older and strikes me as a typical German, with very white skin, but there's no harm in asking: Are you of Brazilian descent? Oh, no, he laughs, unfortunately there is no Brazilian blood in Thuringia, much less in my village, Böhlen. He introduces himself, Wolfgang Probst, and holds out his hand: Welcome. Nice to meet you, I say, Francisco de Hollander, then I invite myself to sit at his table and pour him some wine from my bottle. On the computer screen, he points to a dot on the map showing Thuringia right in the middle of Germany, which with a click is replaced by Brazil, where arrows point from Rio de Janeiro to the interior and south of the country. He says he traipsed all over old coffee plantations in the states of Rio and São Paulo, until he came to Águas Mornas, in Santa Catarina, tracing families from his village that had migrated there in the mid-nineteenth century. In Colônia Santa Isabel he finally found a community of people who had held on to their Thuringian customs and ancestors' surnames. And today he still corresponds with some Probsts, ninth or tenth cousins on the other side of the Atlantic, which is ironic for someone who never even found out what became of his father, Friedrich Probst, lance corporal with the German Army in Normandy just yesterday, in 1944. Still, in spite of his mother, who preferred to believe her husband was dead, he had fantasized from an early age about a deserter living it up in France, remarried and head of a wealthy family, with the name Probst adulterated to Proust for all he knew. Whenever he manages to save a little money, Wolfgang Probst takes a train to Paris, where his favourite pastime is following possible Frédéric Prousts, arm in arm with their madames, down the city's boulevards. Of course he doesn't approach these old men, for if by chance he really were to locate his father, both father and son would find themselves tongue-tied and the game would no longer be fun. In his opinion it would be like a writer finishing a novel that doesn't want to be finished. What about you, have you made any progress in your investigations? I confess that I too am distracted by these unlikely searches, and there is no dearth of people with the surname of my father's girlfriend on the Internet. I have already contacted more than one Sergio Ernst in Germany, another in Portugal, and in Peru, and in Alaska, but I honestly doubt that my brother, at the end of his life, would waste his time on social media. In the future, I might start following some Günthers for a change, if there is any chance that this German couple really did adopt Sergio, even without the required certificates. God only knows, says Wolfgang Probst after examining my letter, but it isn't entirely unthinkable that the authorities turned a blind eye to the fact or made an exception for the little *Mischling*. Because even in the death camps, as it is well known, there were cases of Nazi officials who were so charmed by Jewish children that they smuggled them out, christened them and brought them up as their own. Probst wants to believe that the Günthers were practising Lutherans, like most of the inhabitants of this neighbourhood before communism, and, if so, they would have attended the Immanuel Church, just three blocks from here. He knows Pastor Goertz well and visits the church assiduously, less to participate in the services than as a museologist and researcher. The parish church houses an extensive, centuries-old archive, where there may be some record of the Günther family. And when he sees me looking for the church in my guidebook, Wolfgang Probst tells me the archive isn't open to the public and certain formalities are required in order to consult it: Remember, this isn't Brazil, Mr Hollander. If I agree, he will take note of the Günthers' full address, so that tomorrow morning he can present the pastor with a written request in good German. And night has already fallen when, outside the tavern, he hands me his business card and assures me once again that he has saved the numbers of the Hotel Adlon, my room and my mobile on his phone: Don't worry, Mr Hollander, I'll call as soon as I have any news. You are doing me a great favour, Wolfgang, and, please, feel free to call me Ciccio. As you wish, Mr Ciccio.

The Immanuel Church took no more than forty-eight hours to get back to Wolfgang Probst with the frustrating results of his enquiries. And I, who had been planning to spend a week in Berlin, rebook my ticket home and leave the hotel after three nights, taking nothing more than half a dozen books as souvenirs. I didn't go to libraries, museums, the Opera House, I didn't hire a bike or stroll through the parks, in spite of the springtime sun. I went everywhere by taxi, especially on Kurfürstendamm, or Ku'damm to Berliners and most certainly to Father, who in his youth would have frequented the cafes, theatres and dance halls on the avenue. I went around the corner to Fasanenstrasse 22, Anne Ernst and Heinz Borgart's old address, now the Hotel Augusta, and I had lunch at the house next door, number 23, the literary cafe where Anne posed beside Father with a bulging belly. I tried to guess which boarding house Father stayed at, out of so many in the vicinity of Kurfürstendamm, considerably damaged by the air raids. And if Father could see the glass towers that have gone up here and there, they might look to him like the ghosts of more familiar buildings that were reduced to dust. Not to mention those that have retained only the outer shell of the original, like an ancient jacket on a new book that Father would open, perplexed: Assunta! Assunta! And needless to say I came across a Sergio Ernst on every street corner. On the second day I followed one of them down Ku'damm to the back of a bookshop. There I saw him push his glasses up on his forehead, flick through a book or two, distractedly light a cigarette and look surprised when he was scolded by the sales assistant. It just so happens his name was Sergiusz, Sergiusz Berenbaum, a professor of German-language literature in Warsaw, and he didn't mind being approached by a stranger from South America. On the contrary, he spoke enthusiastically of his essay on Robert Walser in an out-of-print publication, ran on about contemporary authors I'd never heard of and made me buy a handful of books that were hidden from view. When I got back to the hotel, I forced myself to stop by the business centre, to keep on top of my correspondence with the readers of my webpage. I sat next to an Englishwoman in her sixties, whom I greeted with discreet gallantry, but as soon as I typed my password into the computer, the screen was filled with naked women of every description. Out of nowhere there came offers of luxury escorts in Berlin, which I deleted in a hurry, giving way to scenes of sodomy, which were hard to delete, and I only managed to remove a transvestite with a giant cock by unplugging the computer. I put off my work, went up to my room and leaned back on the bed, curious about the new books, perhaps the first in my entire life that I had allowed myself to hold without them having passed through Father's hands. I read a few short poems, I read the blurb on the back of a book of short stories, I took a peek inside a novel filled with photographs of animals, people, train stations, but my attention kept drifting away; I hadn't had any update on my brother for two days. I rang Probst, left a message, turned out the light, turned it back on again, went back to the illustrated novel, and got stuck on page three. I opened a beer, lit a cigarette, decided to try a bit more of the novel, maybe just to the end of the first chapter, but the chapter was endless. There was page after page of a single paragraph which I couldn't leave unfinished, and hours later I was sorry Father hadn't lived long enough to read that book. I was sorry he hadn't lived over a hundred years so that, weary of literature, he might have agreed to read only those novels that I had personally vetted. At dawn I close the book by this author called W.G. Sebald, who in turn closes his book by closing the book of a certain Dan Jacobson, and as I slip into a bad dream I am woken by Wolfgang Probst's call: Arthur Erich Willy Günther and Pauline Anna Günther, maiden name Pohl, really did attend the Immanuel Church, where, on 30 November 1937, they christened their son, Horst. It wasn't Sergio, it was Horst. The name of the adopted boy was Horst.

Horst, I mutter in the taxi, unintentionally, and the driver is surprised to hear me call him by his first name. After Bulgarians, Ghanaians and Afghans, old Horst is the first German taxi driver to pick me up, now that I'm on my way to the airport. He asks if I mind the music, which, absorbed in other thoughts, I hadn't even noticed, and it is a woman singing vigorously: *A hundred times I've cursed Berlin, a hundred times . . .* You probably don't know her, says the driver. It's Helga Hahnemann, a big name back in the days of East Germany. Good voice, I say, but don't tell me she sang the Lipsi too. Horst jests: The Lipsi, the Lipsi, did you know that in 1959, already sick of learning Russian at school, I almost took refuge in West Berlin just to be free of the Lipsi? I'm sorry, are you a musician? No, I say, I teach literature. You're a Turk, aren't you? You've got a Turkish accent. No, sir, I'm Brazilian. Brazilian, Brazilian, I read a Brazilian novel a long time ago, about a woman with two husbands. Ah, yes, *Dona Flor* by Jorge, my late friend Jorge Amado. Amado, says Horst, I bet Amado belonged to the Communist Party. Here in Eastern Europe they published communist authors from all over the world. My taxi driver really wasn't fond of the Russians, or the Lipsi, or the Stasi, or the Wall. But I still consider myself a man of the left, he says, tapping his temple with his index finger: It's a viewpoint, you know. At this instant I feel a kind of vertigo, my vision clouds over, and with a chill I think of Mother, who used to hear voices. The voice I hear is Father's, but to my relief it isn't, what would you call it, a voice from beyond the grave. It is his still-crystalline voice from my childhood. I'll be damned if it isn't Father singing on Helga Hahnemann's record: *The grandparents would sit in front of their houses / At night, in the village, under the lime trees* . . . It is a cheery song, it's got rhythm, but I find it hard to imagine the scholar Sergio de Hollander neglecting his obligations in São Paulo to come and record pop music in Germany: When was this recorded, sir? This recording, I think it's from sixty-something, says Horst, retrieving the CD cover, a compilation of Helga Hahnemann's greatest hits, from the dashboard. And now Helga herself comes on and sings in harmony with Father: *We are sitting in buildings above the cities / In the light, though down below there is already shadow / And we see the stars* . . . I snatch the cover from the driver's hand and run my eyes over the track titles until I reach number 8: *Wir sitzen auf Hochhäusern (Duett mit Sergio Günther)*. Sergio Günther, it says duet with Sergio Günther.

'Hallo!'

'Hallo, Wolfgang? Wolf? I found my brother, can you hear the singer?'

The name rings a bell with Wolfgang Probst, who I find installed in the smokers' room of the Adlon, with a glass of white wine and his laptop open on the table. While he was waiting for me he made a few phone calls and of course looked up Sergio Günther on the Internet, who appears among others with the same name in Switzerland, Australia, India and even Joinville, in Brazil. Probst read up about Günther, mostly repeated information, with no up-to-date details or images of the artist. But from what he can see, in addition to recording LPs and compact singles, Günther worked in the 1960s and 1970s as master of ceremonies on TV music programmes, for which he also conducted interviews and produced news segments in his native Germany as well as Eastern bloc countries. At that time Wolfgang Probst still lived out in the provinces and didn't see much television. But his companions at the Vinería Carvalho are Berliners, most of whom grew up in that very same neighbourhood, and it's possible that, as young people, they may not only have watched the programmes, but also have seen the Günther family out and about. As such, they would be in a position to confirm if the Günthers' son and the famous artist were the same person. Wolfgang Probst doesn't buy this theory, lest he lose faith in the Immanuel Church's archives. He thinks the singer is more likely the child of Catholic Günthers, who named their son Sergio after some saint. Bertolt, Theodor, Johannes, Hermann, Elias, Jacob, Wilhelm, Probst's friends, actually did remember seeing Sergio Günther on TV, whether reading one of Rilke's poems, presenting a Romanian Dixieland band or singing tangos to an elegantly dressed auditorium. But according to Rainer, who was born at 20 Greifswalder Strasse, practically opposite 212/13, the old factory has been abandoned for as long as he can remember. Nevertheless, he gave Wolfgang Probst the number of his cousin Winfried, a cameraman who must have worked with Sergio Günther at the TV studio. But no, Winfried said he had only started the job in 1981, by which time Sergio Günther had taken leave from the studio for health reasons. The cameraman did, however, unearth a phone number for Gottfried, an old-school cinematographer, who, sadly, died three years ago, according to his widow, Ingeborg. It was she who put Probst in touch with Robinson, a retired journalist, who had worked with both Gottfried and Sergio Günther. Now we are already glancing at each other restlessly, Probst and I, because it is well after the appointed hour, when a man in puffy trousers and braces, without a jacket, strolls into the room, unhurried, glancing about at those present. Probst and I both stand at the same time to shake his hand, and after a moment's hesitation Robinson smiles at me: Wolfgang Probst? Greying, on the plump side, with a kindly manner, Robinson reminds me of someone but I don't know who. With age we lose the ability to recognize people, perhaps due to the accumulation of faces printed onto our retinas, and there isn't a new one that doesn't vaguely remind us of another. Always smiling, he raises his glass to toast with us but doesn't take a sip, holding it mid-air as he speaks slowly. He says he should have come by metro because he lives next door to Schillingstrasse station, but he needed to give the car a run. The hotel's valet didn't look too eager to take it, though, so he had to drive around a bit to find a parking spot. But, as he was saying, he lives ten minutes away from Leninplatz, now United Nations Square, where he used to pick up Sergio Günther, who lived there with the studio's wardrobe mistress. With him at the wheel, Sergio beside him and Gottfried in the back seat with his equipment, they would head off to film their segments in his old banger, which had never been anything to write home about, even in its prime. An opinion, incidentally, not shared by Sergio, in whose mind the other side's BMWs and Porsches were not a patch on our Trabant, although we never really knew if he was being serious or not. There was much drinking and fun to be had on these excursions, and the two of them had only fallen out once, after Robinson had gone to Czechoslovakia in 1968. Sent by *Neues Deutschland* to cover the beetroot harvest, Robinson had returned fascinated with what was being dubbed the Prague Spring. But it wasn't over political differences that they had fought; it was because Sergio had stolen Robinson's girlfriend while he was away, but even so, their friendship prevailed and soon they were back on the road again. As he was saying, the Trabi was a stiff, noisy car, but nonetheless it took them far, belching out smoke all over the Carpathians and the Balkans, especially the Balkans, because Sergio had become obsessed with producing stories in Yugoslavia. A month wouldn't go by without Channel 1 airing a programme about Yugoslavia, to the degree that envious Party members accused Sergio of having affairs with Croatian women. On these international trips, in addition to scripting the segments, Robinson served as interpreter, because Sergio only spoke German. Sergio wasn't a big reader, although he had read Goethe and Schiller at school and had chosen Thomas Mann's confidence man Felix Krull as his literary hero. But his wife, the sound designer, always told him not to leave his notes lying around the studio for anyone to see, as they were full of grammatical errors. Apparently, at about sixteen years of age, Sergio Günther had swapped his studies for the barracks, not because he was particularly keen on a military career, but because he wanted to join the prestigious army choir. Robinson had heard this from someone else, because when he met Sergio he already worked in television and was tight-lipped about his life prior to that. Once, after a few glasses, Sergio told him that he remembered the perfume of a woman who used to visit him when he was a boy, presumably his birth mother. And another night he said that when his father, Arthur, died he took his mother, Pauline, to live with him and Susanne, the journalist he was married to at the time. During the move, he opened a drawer and in so doing discovered the names of his biological parents as well as his own birth name. He understood that the Günthers, even back in the 1930s, had felt it prudent to give him an authentically German name, Horst, to substitute for the Sergio inherited from his Brazilian father. My father, I murmur, and Robinson looks at me without surprise. When Wolfgang Probst asked Robinson to come and talk about Sergio Günther in person, he assumed, given that it was confidential, that he would be talking to his friend's secret son, born perhaps to a Croatian mother, you never know. And I am obviously too old to be Sergio Günther's son, but when he saw me he thought he knew me from somewhere. And the minute I greeted him, he had no doubt that he was standing before Sergio Günther's brother. If he listened to me with his eyes closed, he could have sworn it was Sergio putting on a Turkish accent. What about the colour of his skin, I ask, his mouth, his hair, in what else are we alike? And Robinson, after knocking back his wine in a single gulp, says: Don't you want to see him?

The Academy Award-winning actor Emil Jannings, forty-five, doesn't yet know that Goebbels is going to name him Artist of the State. Marlene Dietrich, twenty-seven, a small-time actress, already knows she is going to be Marlene Dietrich. Here in Potsdam, next door to Berlin, the UFA studios from the early twentieth century live on in the Filmpark Babelsberg. And in this wooden shed, the set from *The Blue Angel* cabaret has been re-built as it was in 1929. Emil Jannings, playing the teacher Rath, perhaps already knows he is going to ruin his life for Lola. Lola, in a suspender belt, crosses her Marlene Dietrich legs: *Men cluster to me / Like moths around a flame / And if their wings burn / I know I'm not to blame / Love's always been my game / Play it how I may* . . . The waltz seeping out through the walls of the shed is well-suited to flirting, and perhaps Father and Anne fall in love without a thought about having a child. And Sergio Günther will work for years on end in the future state television studios, unaware that his story began in the shed next door. Of his mother he will recall a scent, and, according to Robinson, from time to time he will think about trying to contact his father, who is probably a journalist or a diplomat. But due to his busy life and the precarious, if not frowned upon, communications with the West, he will end up deciding it isn't feasible. Just as to me the idea that I might one day find myself in the Filmpark Babelsberg, about to see an almost invented German brother, would have seemed absurd. Nevertheless, after making me wait an eternity, a smiling Robinson will come and find me in the shed, with those braces that, at a glance, remind me of Marlene Dietrich's suspender belt. And my hand will shake slightly as he gives me a visitor's ID to hang round my neck. As we make our way through a maze, Robinson will confess that he was afraid the archive employees wouldn't be able to locate Sergio Günther. But soon we will be sitting in a small projection booth, facing a miniature cinema screen where the TV DRA symbol will flicker. And perhaps my eyes will mist over as they fix on the black-and-white image, on the opposite bank of the river, of my brother Sergio. It's Mimmo, I will think out loud, and beside me Robinson will say: Huh? It will actually occur to me that Sergio Günther is Mimmo himself, at the age of thirty, exiled in East Berlin with a nebulous past and a false name. But as the camera closes in on Sergio, more and more I will see Father's oblong face, bulbous nose and even his glasses. His way of pulling his lips back as he puffs on a cigarette and flicks away the butt will be Father's. And I might be wildly mistaken, or are those my pursed lips I see when he begins to whistle a sad melody, a powerful, precise whistle that few can make as well as me. Then I will want to laugh at the way he walks, like Father and me, not unlike a penguin, to the sound of the Russian chords of an invisible orchestra. And I will feel pleasantly jealous when I see a girl in a full skirt run to meet him, the spitting image of Maria Helena as a young woman. In the end I will recognize from I don't know where the song that he will sing to her on the banks of the Spree: *They say / That somewhere / Maybe in Brazil / There is a happy man.*

Sergio Günther, the son of Sergio Buarque de Holanda and Anne Ernst (or Anne Margrit Ernst, or Annemarie Ernst), was born in Berlin on 21 December 1930. In 1931 or 1932, his mother handed him over to the Secretariat for Childhood and Youth of the district of Tiergarten, Berlin. In 193?, Arthur Erich Willy Günther and his wife, Pauline Anna, adopted the boy, who was raised as Horst Günther. Around the age of twenty-two, Horst discovered the identity of his biological parents and chose to revert to his birth name, Sergio. He enlisted in the German Democratic Republic army in 194? and in the late 1950s got a job with the State Television, where his roles were many. He recorded an uncertain number of records, now out of circulation. He died of cancer on 12 September 1981.

Berlin, den 18.4.   19 35.

Jugendamt, Amtsvormundschaft IV

Turmstr. 70.

C 9 Tierg. 0013, App. 14.

u/Zeichen:
Jug. 2 E. 146.

Herrn
Sergio de Hollander,
Rio de Janeiro.
----

39 Rio Maria Angelika
Südamerika.

Unter Bezugnahme auf mein Schreiben vom 24.
9.1934 bitte ich Sie nochmals zwecks Fest-
stellung der arischen Abstammung unseres Mün-
dels Sergio Ernst, mir Ihre Geburtsurkunde,
die Geburtsurkunden Ihrer Eltern und die Geburtsurkunden Ihrer beiderseitigen Grosel-
tern möglichst bald zu übersenden. Das für
die Adoption zuständige Gericht hat diese
Urkunden verlangt.

I. A. Grieskamp.

Author's Note

I discovered what became of my brother Sergio Günther thanks to the efforts of the historian João Klug and the museologist Dieter Lange. Their research in Berlin was based on the documents in this book, preserved by my mother, Maria Amelia Buarque de Holanda. I was put in touch with Klug and Lange by my editor, Luiz Schwarcz, and the historian Sidney Chalhoub.

In May 2013 I travelled to Berlin with my daughter Silvia Buarque, whose contribution was fundamental in the interviews with Sergio's daughter, Kerstin Prügel, his granddaughter, Josepha Prügel, his ex-wife, Monika Knebel, and his friends Werner Reinhardt and Manfred Schmitz.

Chico Buarque

Illustration Credits

pp. 32, 91, 138, 169–170 and 198: Author's personal archive. Reproduced by Jaime Acioli.

p. 197: DRA–Deutsches Rundfunk archiv. 17 Ausschnitte. Sergio Günther (1961–81). © Robert Lackenbach/The *Life* Picture Collection/ Getty Images.